Inherited Murder:
A Medium with a Heart

Book 4

Erica J Whelton

Publisher: Sunseri Design Publishing
ISBN: 978-1-956069-12-9

Printed in the United States of America

To my Uncle David and Aunt Peggy for always supporting me
and being there for me throughout my life. And also, for giving me my
Treasure Bear when I was two years old.

Books in this series:

Premedicated Murder (book 1)
Replicated Murder (book 2)
Organized Murder (book 3)
Inherited Murder (book 4)
Crafted Murder (book 5)
Destined Murder (book 6)

Other books by this Author:

Mandy's Story: A Glenn Lake Novel (book 1)
Becca's Story: A Glenn Lake Novel (book 2)
Caroline's Story: A Glenn Lake Novel (book 3)

The Haunting of Anna-Rose (Paranormal Suspense)
Decoding Us (Women's Fiction/Friendship)

Chapter One

~ Joanna ~

I was in my office answering emails between client readings. I always had a lot of fan mail to answer. Mostly from people that were happy with their reading, a few had read my book and loved it. Then there were others who shared their own paranormal experiences with me.

It was always fun to read each and every one. It was one of my favorite perks of this job.

Commotion near the door broke my focus. I looked up to see two older people standing there. The man and woman were whispering back and forth, oblivious to the fact I was now staring at them.

"I heard she can see us now," he said.

"But how will we know if she can?" she said.

"I don't know. Do we just ask her?"

"I don't want to scare her."

Clearly, they were spirits, as my door was closed and they hadn't opened it. With my concentration broken, I decided I would stop their bickering and settle their debate.

"I can see AND hear you."

They jumped at my voice.

"See." He mumbled.

"Oh, we're sorry to intrude, dear. It's just we heard that you could help people like us." She giggled. "People, you know, the dead ones."

"Yeah, I got that," I said flatly as I looked at them more closely. "You both look so familiar, but I can't quite put my finger on how I know you."

"Well, not me, dear. I was just an old woman that cleaned houses most of my life." She nodded towards the man. "But you might have known him."

"Arnold Crawford."

"Oh my, Senator Crawford?" I stammered.

He nodded.

Arnold Crawford was from old money and one of the country's wealthiest families. His grandfather, or maybe a great grandfather, discovered oil on their family land, which set them up to establish their own oil and gas company. After that, they branched out into real estate, restaurants, and many other businesses.

"Well, okay, how can I help you?" I sat forward.

"We need to get a message to our son," He said.

"Your son?"

"Hank Hammersley." She said.

"I'm sorry. Did you say your son is Hank the Hammer?" I asked. "Are you Hedy?"

"You've heard of me?"

"I have. He asks about you often, but I didn't know..." I gestured towards Arnold. "He never mentioned."

"He doesn't know. We never told him." She said.

"It's a complicated story. My family didn't approve and made things, well, difficult to say the least." Arnold said.

"Okay." My mind was spinning. How would Hank take this news? "But how are you both..."

"Dead? That's a good question." He lowered his voice. "To be honest, I think we might have been murdered."

He looked over at Hedy. She simply nodded.

"Wait, murdered?" I wish I had some popcorn because this story was about to get good. Juicy gossip was a fun perk of this job.

"Yes, and before I tell you our theory, we want to ask your help in warning Hank because we think he might be next."

Forget the popcorn. I needed a stiff drink. This sounded more like a hot mess than it did juicy gossip, and like I would soon be putting myself in some awkward situations. Not to mention, Hank's reaction to this news. I knew he would be happy to speak to his mother, but how would he take the rest of this story?

"Warn him, how? About what?" I stammered.

"Well, as I'm sure you know, I have or had a lot of money." He frowned. "My family can't access it because I left it to our son, Hank. Only his name isn't Hank in my will because his real name isn't Hank."

"What?" I blurted, then slapped my hand over my mouth. I hated when I slipped out of character. I inhaled and tried to refocus on being professional.

"His birth name was Arnold Crawford the second, but I changed it when he was still a baby. Arnie's family made many threats against us and basically paid me off to change his name, keep him a secret, and lie about who the father was." Hedy said. "Obviously, I wanted to protect my son and myself, so I changed his name and took off the father's name, saying I had lied about his identity."

"It was ugly for a while, but since Hedy kept up her end of the bargain, my family soon forgot about it or at least faked it," Arnie said. "I married someone they approved of, and life went on. Hedy got a nice monthly allowance, so I knew at least my son was cared for financially. Plus, they allowed Hedy to keep her job."

"I'm sorry, that had to be tough on all of you, but I don't understand what you need help with now. Just to tell Hank you are his father?"

"Yes and no. The way our estate was set up, one person controls it, and everyone else gets an allowance. At current, nobody in the family can make any changes or take full control."

"That's strange. I've never heard of that."

"Yeah, my great-grandfather set it up this way to protect the fortune. My lawyer had written in my will a clause saying if Hank came forward for the money within two years of my death, he would be the one in control of it. If he doesn't, it will simply be split between my third wife, Irene, my sister, Faye, and my two cousins, Oren and Viola. My wife getting the largest share, followed by my sister, and then my cousins would get what was left. This includes businesses, stocks, bonds, etcetera. All worth close to a billion."

I choked slightly, causing Arnie to chuckle at my slip in professionalism, again, but I recovered quickly.

"Why two years? That's a strange deadline."

"Yeah, that's what my lawyer said too, but that was how long I got to be in his life before... before I had to deny him, and Hedy changed his name. He was Arnie the second for two years, and then when he was about four or five, they had to move away." His voice choked.

"I don't understand. I thought that your family wanted you to deny him?" I asked.

"It's true, but since Hedy was still working for us at the time, I could see him and spend time with him, at least at first. He was the cutest little guy toddling around after me." Arnie said.

"He loved you so much," Hedy added with a smile.

They stared at each other as if sharing the memory telepathically. Their moment had me feeling like a third wheel.

"Sorry, but back to the story, that's why I picked two years. I know it seems strange, but you can make quirky requests when you have enough money." He chuckled. "People don't question you, at least not to your face, and just say 'yes, sir.'"

"Why now? I thought you passed nearly two or maybe three years ago. Isn't the deadline over then?"

"Yes, almost two years, and we are running out of time. Only a few more months left for him to come forward."

"Okay, but why now? Why not when you were first killed?" I might actually know the answer to this one. "Oh, because I was faking it then?"

"Yes, that, and then we didn't know until recently that you had real powers," Hedy said. "We heard what you did for your husband, so here we are."

"You heard it through the ghost-vine?" I chuckled. It was a term a spirit had told me once. Unfortunately, she had been a victim of the Playhouse Killer.

"The what?" They asked in unison.

"Never mind. Just a bad joke."

"So, will you help us?" Arnie asked.

I stared at their hopeful faces for a moment. Each time one of these murder mysteries presented itself, I wanted to pretend I really couldn't see the dead anymore. But, on the flip side, I was so curious and wanted to see how it turned out. I loved the suspense and adrenaline rush it gave me.

Not to mention, I loved helping people. It gave them closure which was my whole brand, and my own need for closure took me on this journey.

"Yes, I'll do it."

At that moment, Tessa buzzed my phone to let me know my next appointment had arrived. I thanked her.

"We will get out of your way now but will be back soon to talk details." Hedy said. "Thank you so very much."

They waved as they walked through the wall. I sat there for a moment, staring at the spot.

This one sounded like it would get messy, and money always brought out the worst in people, like murder.

"What did I just agree to?" I sighed and went to my next reading.

Chapter Two

~ Joanna ~

"Come on, Oakie, you've got this." I held my hands out for my daughter. At only nine months old, she was on the verge of walking. I knew she was early, but she seemed ready, so I was simply encouraging her. Though I knew she would do it in her own time.

She let go of the couch and giggled as she plopped on her diapered butt and crawled to me.

"Well, that's one way." I scooped her up and kissed her head. "You'll do it when you're ready."

She giggled and planted a raspberry on my cheek.

"Aw, thanks for the slobbery kiss, baby." I wiped my cheek with a laugh.

My phone rang.

"Hey, Clint."

"Hey, Jo. Mind if I stop by?"

"Come on over."

Things between us had been hot and heavy for a while after my last murder investigation. Though technically, I was a medium and not a detective. Like with Arnie and Hedy, ghosts would ask me for favors, so I tried to do the best I could for them. So far, I was three for three.

The last was my ex-husband, and it turns out his own parents killed him, though indirectly. In the process of that investigation, I had been shot, and they had been killed.

The leg injury was a small price to pay for the closure that solving that gave me. Despite all the deceit and problems he had caused me, I felt awful for Ted in a way. To find out you had been killed by your own parents' order is just sad.

Clint and I have been in an on-again-off-again relationship for the past year. After I was shot, we were on again. While I recovered, he'd temporarily moved in to help with the baby as she still required a lot of care that I couldn't do on crutches.

Now that I was mostly recovered, he had moved back home. We were still a couple, just living separately, but I recently felt he was pulling back again. We hadn't spoken much this past week or two. I blamed my being back at work and us not being in the same house, but in my gut, it felt like something else.

There was a knock at my door.

"That must be Clint." Chewy, my dog, started barking and spinning his way towards the door. Oakley giggled and crawled after him. I followed the crazy parade, and as the other two couldn't, I opened the door wide. "Hey, join the party."

But my joy at seeing him was short-lived, as his stiff expression had me second-guessing this visit.

"Da!" Oakley exclaimed.

"Oh, my." He bent over to pick her up. "Did she just call me...?"

"It sounded like it, but honestly, she's been calling everyone and everything da." I let out a guarded laugh. "Well, come on in. Want a drink? I think I have a beer or two."

"No, I'm not staying long."

"Oh-kay." I closed the door and followed him into the living room.

He was tickling Oakley and asking her about her day. She babbled away. Like with walking, she was on the cusp of talking, and you could hear words mixed in with the rambling.

Chewy was panting and whimpering next to Clint, waiting on his turn for attention.

"Oh, hi, boy. Aren't you a good boy?" He finally said as he gave Chewy scratches behind his ears.

The big mutt rolled over on his back, happy for the attention. Clint then looked at me, and his expression fell.

"What is going on with you? You seem off."

"Sorry." He tried to smile.

"Well, something is bothering you. Is it me? Did I do something?"

"Not exactly, but..." He sighed heavily. "There is an internal investigation starting at work."

"Why?"

"Because of how we have handled, or I should say, mishandled some of the murder cases." He paused. "Thanks to you."

"Me?"

"Yes, all your medium voodoo has the powers that be looking through all of our cases. Terry and I are in a lot of trouble right now."

"I'm sorry. I wasn't trying to..."

"Of course not, but you didn't think about that when you started poking your nose in those cases. Your actions have real consequences." He snapped.

That pissed me off. How dare he say it like I'm a bad guy. I was simply trying to help.

"Yeah, but I helped you, and I helped those people get closure." I sat up straighter. "I also stopped a serial killer. Actually, if you think about it, a couple of them."

"But now my job is on the line. I could be fired or maybe even arrested."

That stopped my anger from flaring further.

"Arrested? Why?"

"If they think I did it on purpose, then yes."

"Clint, I'm so sorry. I just wanted to help, and if you remember, you and Terry came to me about the Playhouse Killer."

He continued to pet Chewy as he stared at me. The baby was sitting in his lap playing with his sunglasses, completely unaware that we were fighting.

"Yeah, okay, that one. But with the Landon case, we had closed it, and then bam, three murders. Two that we botched the investigation on."

"I can keep apologizing, but honestly, I'm not sorry for solving that. I got Caitlin off the street and got her the help she desperately needed. Granted, she is about to spend the rest of her life in prison, but I think she finally has closure and a happier outlook in general."

"I just... I can't believe I messed up so much. Renee's death was one of my first cases, and then when Jeremy died the same way, it just seemed like an identical accident." He sighed and covered his face with his hands. "I thought I was ready to be a detective, but truthfully, it's a lot harder than I thought."

I moved closer to him, taking one of his hands. He looked up at me and flashed a wounded smile.

"So, what're the next steps with the internal stuff?" I asked.

"They dig into all the cases Terry and I have worked. See if they can find mistakes, missteps, etcetera."

I wanted to mention the visit from Arnie and Hedy. If they had been murdered, I had no idea if there was even merit to their claims. I hadn't even started researching it yet. Were those cases he had worked on?

"I can't remember, when did you start?"

"Being a detective?" I nodded in reply, so he continued. "Not quite three years ago."

"Did you work on the Arnie Crawford case?" I couldn't help myself. I had to know.

"The Senator? No, if I remember correctly, he died in Centerville. Someone over there would have investigated it." He said, but then glared at me. "Why?"

"Oh, no reason." I picked up Oakley from his lap. Yes, I was using my daughter as a kind of shield.

"Jo, spill it." His dark eyes flared. It would be sexy if it wasn't from anger at me.

I didn't want to tell him and wish I would have kept my mouth shut, but that was not a trait I possessed. My curious side always took over, and I'd ask one too many questions or say something that I shouldn't have.

"Okay, fine. Arnie, along with Hedy, Hank's mom, came to see me earlier today."

"And? Let me guess, they claim he was murdered."

"They both were."

"You've got to be kidding me." He pushed himself up from the floor onto the couch. "And let me guess, they don't know who did it or how."

"Well, sort of. They think it was someone in his family, but not sure who."

"Unbelievable." He stood and started pacing. "Our department handled Hedy's. Thankfully it wasn't me. And as I said, the Senator's happened in Centerville, so their department handled that. So I should be in the clear on this one."

"I don't know if it is anything or not. I haven't even started looking into it yet."

"Are you going to?"

"I wanted to talk to Hank first, but depending on how that goes, then yes."

"Can you promise that you'll come to me with anything you find and that you please, please stay safe?"

"Yes, of course." I didn't know that I could honestly promise those things, but I would do my best to try for him.

"Great."

He took Oakley from me, and they played ball with Chewy for the rest of his short visit. I quietly observed from the sidelines. I knew it was valuable for her to have different people in her life, and she loved this person.

As I walked him to the door, he finally smiled at me.

"I'm sorry for being grumpy. Just work stress." He said, pulling me in for a goodbye kiss. "I promise next time I'll try to be in a better mood."

"Things will be okay, even if they don't feel like it now."

"Yeah... I'll try to remember that." He kissed me once more before walking away, waving before getting into his truck and driving away.

I sighed. I knew I would stick my nose too far into this case, but I had to find a balance that kept me safe and didn't make it look as if he wasn't a good detective. Plus, like he said, he didn't work these cases, so any backlash wouldn't hurt him, right?

Chapter Three

~ Joanna ~

This morning, my first thoughts were about Clint's visit last night. With his cold demeanor towards me, I was relieved when he left. He seemed a bit depressed, or perhaps there was resentment towards me.

Though he apologized for his mood, it didn't completely remove the pain it caused me. I'd laid awake thinking about him and concerned for his job too.

It wasn't like I had meant to hurt him. I was just helping people who needed it. My desire for closure is what drove me to want to give that to others. It didn't matter if they were alive or dead. I just wanted to help people.

Today, I would try to bring that peace to two such souls, Arnie and Hedy. I didn't know how Hank would feel about all of this, but I hoped it would bring him some comfort as well.

Over the last year, when I would see him, he asked about his mother. I got the impression that it was more than just missing her that had him asking. Perhaps he had some suspicion that her death wasn't what it looked like.

I didn't do my usual prework research for this. I knew that I wouldn't find anything on Hank. He kept a low profile online. I already knew a lot from the news about Senator Crawford. Anything I found would be news articles and tabloid stories. For now, I didn't think it would help, but it was always an option later.

Instead, I would need to speak with Hank. He needed to and deserved to know that his mother had been in touch. So I sent a text message to his number two guy, Al. He always set up the meetings between us when I needed. I didn't tell him why I wanted to speak to Hank, just that I did. His reply was instant.

Not today. Thursday.

That was all he said. I let him know that Thursday would work. I had to work around Hank's schedule, not the other way around, so it didn't matter. Though I knew without looking, I still pulled up my calendar to see how my day looked on Thursday.

"Ugh, full day." Not really surprising.

Without a time, I'd have to block the entire day, which meant asking Tessa to rearrange and reschedule those appointments.

I was overdue for a day off anyway. Perhaps I'd give Janie the day off and spend most of the day with Oakley. Audrey could possibly babysit while I was meeting with Hank, but I'd figure that part out later.

Waiting until Thursday also allowed me to try reconnecting with Arnie and Hedy. But unfortunately, they hadn't been back in several days, and of course, I had no way to get in touch with them.

Since we hadn't planned for when I'd talk to Hank or start investigating this, I was stuck until they came back to me.

Arnie had only mentioned his family, but he didn't give me much about motive or who he thought it could be. The day they visited, they were mostly focused on Hank.

I looked at the picture of Oakley that I kept on my desk. I understood being more concerned for your child than yourself.

I walked out to the reception area to talk to Tessa.

"Hey, Tessa."

"Hey. Your next appointment isn't here yet."

"Oh, good." I looked around. There were a few dead people, likely waiting on their loved ones to come in. I smiled at them. "I was going to see if we could reschedule my appointments for Thursday."

"I'm sure we can. Let me take a look." She clicked around the computer, pulling up my schedule. "Wow, busy day. Why do you need to cancel?"

I hesitated a moment. After putting myself in harm's way three times in the name of investigating murders, my family and friends had made various threats if I did it again.

"Oh, no, what are you into now?" She said, folding her arms over her chest.

"Hank's mom came to visit me and wants me to do a reading between them. Al didn't confirm the time, so I need the whole day blocked for now. I'll spend the rest of the day with Oakley."

There. That was the truth, just not all of the truth. I'd tell her when I knew more.

"That's wonderful news. Hank's been asking about her." She nodded. "I'll get these moved around."

"Thanks, you're a lifesaver as always."

I looked around once more to make sure Hedy and Arnie weren't here. Still not here, so I went back to my office to get ready for my next appointment.

"Oh, Hedy, hi," I said, seeing her as I walked in.

"Hi, sorry to startle you, but I wanted to talk more about Hank without Arnie here."

"I was just talking to my assistant. I'm going to meet him on Thursday and was hoping you would stop by before then."

"Oh, that's wonderful. What time, and I will, obviously, be with you?"

"I'm not sure a time yet, but let me see if Al messaged me back." I picked up my phone. "Not yet, but I'm sure they will give me a time soon."

She nodded. "I guess I'll need to stick around a bit, so I know when we need to go if that's okay?"

"Sure. I have appointments, so I'll be in and out, but you're more than welcome to hang out."

She sighed and looked around. I didn't have time to speak to her further because Tessa called back, letting me know my appointment was here.

"I'll be back shortly." I smiled at Hedy and walked out. I caught movement over my shoulder as I saw her following me. "Are you coming?"

"Yes, dear. You told me I could hang out. It will be boring in there." She gestured towards my office. "A reading sounds a lot more fun. I can watch you work."

"Okay."

I wasn't sure this was a good idea, but I would go along with it because what choice did I have? She was a ghost, after all, and could go wherever she wanted. So many times, I did readings with extra spirits hanging around. It was just how this thing worked sometimes.

I went to the reception area to call back the Joneses. They were a middle-aged couple dressed to the nines. Him in navy blue slacks and a crisp shirt with a gray cashmere sweater over it. His shoes were black leather and, if I was correct, cost more than my entire outfit today, including my bra and panties.

She was dressed in skin-tight black jeans with a pale pink, silky tunic. She'd paired it with taupe heels and two long silver necklaces.

Of course, it was a simple look, but a trained eye knew her outfit was worth more than my car payment.

They looked so familiar, but I couldn't quite put my finger on it.

Hedy gasped. "That's Oren and Viola. They are Arnie's cousins."

That's right. I tried to hide my surprise as I led them to the room I did readings in. It had comfortable chairs and a large cushy couch. There was soft music playing, scented candles, and lots of tissue boxes. I tried to make it a comfortable, inviting place. The readings could be emotional, so I thought a homelike environment would help relax everyone.

However, I felt I was about to be ambushed by these clients, and I knew Hedy was right because it clicked after she said that. They were in the news a lot, though I'd never been up close and personal with them, and some people looked different in person than in pictures.

They were often referred to as the Odd Crawfords or the Weird Crawfords. They were siblings and always together, and most of the time dressed alike or at least complimentary. Not today, though.

"Alright, Mr. and Mrs. Jones." I paused. "Sorry, I didn't catch your first names."

They exchanged a look that I couldn't quite read.

"I'm Oren, and she's Viola. We're actually not the Joneses. We're Crawfords."

"You've probably seen us in the news," Viola added.

"Ah, I see. Why the false pretenses?" I knew but wanted to see what they'd say.

"As you know, we are important people." Viola paused. I guess waiting for my reaction. When I didn't give one, she huffed but continued. "Our family owns much of this town as well as Centerville and Appleton."

"Of course."

"And we couldn't very well tip people off that we were coming to see a medium. What would they think? I mean, we had to shake the paparazzi from following us here." She flipped her hair. "Oh, no offense."

"None taken." Lots taken, but alright. I just smiled through the insult.

"Plus, how do we know this is all real?" Oren said. Viola nodded and narrowed her eyes on me.

Highly insulted now, I really wanted to ask them to leave, but honestly, this could be the best research I could get.

"Well, okay, let me start by telling you that when I channel your loved ones, I will speak as if they are speaking. This way, you hear their message exactly as they intend it. I don't add or edit what they say in any way." I paused. "Do you have any questions before we start?"

They shook their heads. I wish I could stall more because looking around at the dead people in the room, there wasn't anyone speaking up for them except Hedy, and all I could hear was her cursing them out. It was a bit distracting, but I had gotten somewhat used to all the spirits having side conversations.

"Joanna, since nobody else is stepping forward, what if I fake being their grandmother?" Hedy finally said to me.

I see what she is going for here. Unfortunately, I couldn't acknowledge her directly, so I did the next best thing.

I slightly nodded. "Yes, let me see... Ah, your grandmother has come forward."

"Our grandmother?"

"Yes, but you called her Tootie."

"You could have heard that on the news," Viola said.

"Or read it online," Oren added.

I had heard of Tootie Crawford. Everyone had. Her real name was Theodora Crawford, but I didn't know that even her grandchildren called her by her famous nickname.

"Well, if I wasn't Tootie, would I know that you, Oren, wet the bed until you were 10 years old." I tried to hide my surprise as I spoke Hedy's words. "And, Viola, would I know how you used to sneak off with the gardener's son, Efrain?"

They both gasped and looked wide-eyed at each other. I had to admit she was good. I bet those could be stories on a show or in a book, like confessions of a housekeeper or something. I'd have to see if that was already a thing.

"Tootie?" Oren said. "But, wow, I thought we would get to talk to Arnie. Don't we get to pick who we talk to?"

"That's not exactly how it works. I can only channel the spirit that presents itself, and Tootie is who we have here today." I smiled at Hedy. I would have to remember to thank her for her quick thinking.

"Okay, well, maybe you can help us anyway," Oren said and looked at Viola.

"Arnie has locked up our inheritance. Tommy Jenkins, the family lawyer, says Arnie's son gets it. But we all know Arnie and Irene never had children. His first wife died in childbirth, as did that baby. And he wasn't married to the second one very long. So, who is this random person?" Viola said.

"And nobody would call those brats of Irene's his children. They were mutts from her second marriage." Oren said.

Ouch. That's rude, but I didn't say anything. I would go all mama bear on anyone who called my child a mutt. I wonder what Irene would do if she was here. I heard she had a hot temper.

"It doesn't matter," I said for Hedy.

"Doesn't matter?"

"No, doesn't matter. I know all about the terms. This person is running out of time to come forward, and if he hasn't by now, he never will." I was impressed with Hedy's improvisations.

Oren and Viola looked at each other. He shrugged, and she nodded as if having a telepathic conversation. My sister and I could have similar mental conversations, so I completely understood this sibling bond.

"I guess you're right," Viola said, but her eyes narrowed on me again. "But it would ease our minds if we simply knew that this was all fake and we could collect what's ours."

"You will just have to trust me. This will all work as it's supposed to."

"Okay, thanks, Tootie." They both said.

We finished up the fake reading minutes later. As they left, they seemed mildly satisfied. Thank goodness that Hedy knew so much about their family. Clearly, she had been around them long enough to know dark secrets. I needed to keep her around for any time I was in a jam.

After I walked them out, I went back to my office. I saw that Al had messaged.

"Al says 10 a.m. on Thursday."

"Alrighty, then. I will meet you there." Hedy said and then disappeared through the wall.

Chapter Four

~ Clint ~

The internal investigation had been going on for the past week, and I felt both angry and vulnerable. They were digging through everything, and my partner, Terry, and I were spending our days answering questions and going piece by piece through each of our cases. It was exhausting.

I hadn't spoken to Joanna in all this time and couldn't bring myself to right now. She had brought out an issue that could get me fired. I knew I couldn't hide forever. I would either have to learn to forgive or end things with her. Neither seemed like a good option right now.

I loved that woman and could see a future with her. The first time I've seen a future with anyone since Monica. I sighed as I tried to recall what Mo looked like. Lately, I was forgetting her more than remembering.

Grabbing my phone, I pulled up the last picture we'd taken together. It was the only one I had on my phone. I kept it as a reminder of how short life could be, even though I saw it in my line of work nearly every day.

Her bright smile used to melt my heart. But looking at her familiar face now, she seemed almost like a far-off dream.

I stared at her, wondering what she would be like today. What would our lives be like together? Would we be happy, have kids? I'd never know.

I sighed and put the phone away.

Next, I stared at my computer screen. Nothing was pulled up. Without any cases to work, I had no reports to file and nothing to review. I was simply waiting on them to tell me I was fired or perhaps even arrest me, but my hope was they would hand me a case file and let me get back in the field.

"Hey." My partner, Terry, said at my office door. He came in, plopping down in my other chair. "This sucks."

"Yeah, I hate it."

"I wish they would just tell us something."

I nodded. "I've started looking for another job."

He sat forward. "Do you think we're at that point?"

"I don't know, but I have to do something."

"Yeah, so what are you looking at doing?"

"Bus driver, maybe. Work at one of the home improvement stores. I've looked at a few construction jobs." I shrugged. "What would you do?"

"I really don't know. I love this job."

"Me too." I sighed.

We sat there lost in thought.

He was a bit older and had spent several years in the military before joining the force. We'd first met back in the police academy and were partnered when we graduated. We moved through the ranks together.

There was an almost instant friendship between us as well as a rivalry. Together, we made each other better, pushing each other to do more, be stronger, smarter.

"It was really only the Landon case that we missed signs on and then the serial killer one that we got help from Joanna. So, it wasn't like all of our cases were messed up." Terry said, sitting forward.

"I know, or at least not until Jo tells us some spirit came to her, and all of our cases were botched."

I thought about what Joanna said about Arnold Crawford and Hedy Hammersley, but no point in telling Terry. We hadn't worked on either of those cases, so even if this became murder, we weren't involved.

"Well, I hope that doesn't happen." He exhaled and sat back again. "I just don't think we failed more than that. Do you?"

"I don't know what to think. Their questions have me second-guessing everything in my life." I stared down at my hands. "I just love this job, and I can't picture myself doing anything else."

"Yeah, this is all I ever wanted to do."

I looked over at the time.

"Lunch?"

"Sure."

At least it would break up the monotony of the day. So, we headed over to our favorite place, or at least my favorite, Quench. It was comforting with my current mood to be somewhere I didn't have to think or have pressures on me.

"Hey, Clint, Terry." Angel, the hostess, said with a bright smile. "Chris isn't working, but you want to sit in Marta's section?"

"That works," I said.

We were greeted by staff and a few customers as we made our way to our table. I could feel my mood improving. This was what I needed, to be out of the office, if only for an hour.

We were seated, then ordered our drinks and food. Marta wasn't as talkative as Chris was, but I still liked her. I wasn't much of a talker myself.

Terry got a text from his wife. He smiled. "She wants me to tell you hi."

"Hi to Whitney," I said.

He typed out a message to her. I felt a bit like a third wheel, and she wasn't even here. My cell phone was in my pocket, and I almost sent Joanna a message but decided not to.

I didn't have anything to say with no news from the internal review and no date plans for us. So instead, I looked at my partner as he read the most recent text from his wife. He smiled and then replied.

With him busy at the moment, I scanned the restaurant. Citizens of Creekview that I was sworn to protect, that I wanted to protect even though my job was to investigate after something happened. Still, I wore the badge with pride.

I would happily go back to working as a patrol officer or beat cop, any job if it meant getting to keep that badge and help the people of the town I loved.

Marta brought our food, and we got down to the business of eating. That barbecue bacon burger never tasted so good as it did as a distraction from my problems. But soon, too soon, it was time to head back to the worry box, which is what I had started to call my office.

When we returned to the office, we were called in for yet another round of interviews and more briefs about our cases. Again, they went through fact after fact and clue after clue.

"How did this woman know the details of this case?" An investigator asked.

"She claims to be able to speak to the dead," I said flatly and looked over at my lawyer. He simply nodded. We'd already talked in length about her. He'd advised me to be as honest as possible.

As if I had a choice, I thought with an internal eye roll.

"Do you believe that?"

"Honestly, I don't know."

"Did you provide her details of the case?"

"Limited and with approval."

"So, she could have figured it out from the reports?"

"She seemed to already have the idea about it before reviewing the file."

It was like this for hours. I never wavered. They were trying to determine if I had conspired with her to help her business. I hadn't, and honestly, I still wasn't sure I believed in her powers.

Though it was hard to dispute the results. Like when she told me that Marcus had died at the lab, we had only just arrived there ourselves to start the investigation. The media didn't even know at that point, yet she knew.

She'd said he came with Jeremy Landon. How could she have known that unless she truly was speaking with the dead victim?

Still, my logical, rational brain couldn't process this voodoo magic being true. Instead, I was about facts and evidence.

My head was spinning by the end of the day, and so was my stomach. So, I headed to the gym to burn off some of this stress and frustration.

First, I did five miles on the treadmill. Then, since it was arm day, I ran through my lifting routine before joining some others on the basketball court for a few rounds.

"In your face, Hartley!" One guy yelled as he did a perfect layup.

"I'll catch up, Locke."

It was back and forth with points, but in the end, his team beat mine.

"Better luck next time," Locke called as we all went in different directions.

Physically exhausted and mentally fatigued, I headed home for a shower, a beer, and Monday night football. Overall, not the worst of days, considering my job and reputation were on the line. But at least I could still look at myself in the mirror without cringing.

I'd just keep focusing and answering the questions to the best of my ability and as honestly as possible. That was all I could do.

Chapter Five

~ Joanna ~

I stepped into Leo's ten minutes early. I quickly scanned the bar to see if I saw Hedy and Arnie, but I didn't see either of them.

"Jo!" Eddie yelled as he ran to me. He grabbed me up into a big bear hug.

"Hey, Eddie," I said with a giggle.

"Joanna." Darius called from behind the bar. "Vodka cranberry?"

"It's 10 in the morning."

"Never too early for vodka, and it has juice in it." He laughed.

Eddie finally put me down. "What brings you in today?"

"I have a meeting with Hank."

"An investigation?" Eddie asked.

He had helped me on a few of them, but I didn't know if I wanted to involve any of Hank's men if I didn't have to, especially not before speaking to Hank.

"No, not right now."

At that moment, Al waved me over to Hank's table, so I told the two guys goodbye and took the drink Darius insisted I have with me. I looked around again for Hedy or Arnie. Still not here. So, I'd have to start without them.

"Hello, Ms. Joanna, please have a seat."

"Thank you." I sipped my drink, stalling a moment.

"So, you requested a meeting with me. What's going on? Is it my mother?" He looked around, hopeful.

"Actually, yes, though she isn't here at the moment. She's supposed to meet me here." I scanned the room again, trying in vain to make her materialize.

"You've spoken to her?" He sat forward.

"I have."

"I'm here, dear. I'm here." I finally heard Hedy.

"Oh, good, she's here."

"Mother? You're here?" Hank's eyes lit up like I had never seen.

His usual hard, stone-cold mob boss look was replaced with soft eyes and a bright smile.

It was clear he loved and missed his mother. I was so happy that I was finally going to be able to reconnect them, if only through me.

"Yes, she is. Her exact words were, I'm here, dear." I smiled. "Now, before I go forward, I want to let you know that I will be speaking exactly her words from this point forward."

"I understand." He frowned slightly but then smiled. "Mother, I miss you on Sundays the most. Your roast chicken and rice were the best."

"I'm so glad you enjoyed those meals. I tried to make everything with love." I smiled at Hedy.

She had moved to Hank's side. She tried touching him but couldn't. My vision blurred for a moment as tears formed. I blinked to clear them.

"I don't understand what happened to you that day. The police said you started a fire while cooking, but it appeared you fell down the stairs. If you were cooking downstairs, why were you upstairs? What happened?"

"I honestly don't remember that day well. But I remember starting to cook myself some eggs, nothing fancy. There was a sound in the next room, and next thing I know, I was wandering in the spirit world."

"Then why did you and Arnie think you were murdered?" I said and then instantly regretted it.

"What?" Hank said. "Did my mother say that? Who is Arnie?"

"I'm sorry. She didn't say that. I did, and I shouldn't have."

"We might as well tell him everything." She said.

"Are you sure?"

"Am I sure about what?" Hank asked.

"Sorry, I was speaking to your mother. She says I need to tell you the full story."

"Full story?"

"Yes, and this might be hard to hear. But first, I will ask, do you have any doubts that what I do is fake?"

He thought for a moment. "Are you telling me you are faking this?"

"No, gawd, no. I just want to ensure or do whatever is necessary before I tell you the full story so that you believe that I'm not making this up."

"Okay, um, here is one. What was the song you always sang to me when I was down?"

"Over the rainbow from the Wizard of Oz," I said for Hedy.

"That's right. One more question, what was our first dog's name?"

"Polka Dot, but we called her Dot or Dottie. We only called her Polka Dot when she was naughty, like when she ate the volcano you'd built for the science fair." I smiled at that. It was a sweet name.

"She was a good dog, even if she destroyed all that work." He chuckled. "I believe. Now, what is going on with my mother?"

"Alright, well, your birth name is actually," I paused and lowered my voice, "Arnold Crawford the second."

"What?" His voice roared, and he flew out of the booth. Passing right through Hedy in the process.

He started pacing back and forth. Muttering as he stomped around, but I couldn't understand him. Hedy followed him, wringing her hands and muttering to him. Not that he could hear her.

As they always did when Hank got angry, his men stopped what they were doing to ensure there was no threat. All eyes went to me. A few realized and laughed it off.

He came back over but didn't sit.

"So, you're telling me that I'm the son of Senator Arnold Crawford."

"Yes."

"Son of a..." He finally sat again. "I don't understand what this has to do with how my mother died or was murdered, or whatever."

He started rubbing his temples. I had never seen him so unglued. He was always so composed and never let his emotions show unless he was trying to intimidate someone, but that was anger.

"He died a month or so before I did, and he remembers being at home, but like me, not much else."

"How is that even possible that you can't remember? Wouldn't it be a big deal, a big moment?"

"You would think, but one minute you are alive, and the next there is this weird peace." I smiled at Hedy and added, "I've heard that from other spirits. Unfortunately, not many of them remember the moments leading up to and right after death."

Hank looked from me to the spot I was staring. He then reached out towards where Hedy was, his hand going through her. She smiled and reached for him too.

I just watched in awe. It was a sweet moment between mother and son, even if they couldn't themselves see it or feel it.

"Okay, so let me get this straight, Ms. Medium, you are telling me my birth name is Arnold Crawford the second, so why was my name changed? Why was this all a secret?"

"She was the housekeeper for the Crawford family for many years," I said.

"And tell him that my mother was before me."

I repeated it.

"Okay, but..." he gasped. "Does that mean...?"

"Yes, I was having a fling with the Senator, and his family found out. Having money, they had power, which in turn meant controlling their son's life. So they paid me off, and I had to change your birth certificate and name. I was allowed to continue to work for the family for a few more years, but in time, I quit, and we moved here to Creekview to be away from the Crawfords in Centerville."

"Now that you mention it, I do remember you working for them and us living in that tiny house outback, but the memory is kind of fuzzy."

"Yes, but as you got older, I wanted different for you, and you were starting to look like Arnie. So, it was time for us to move on. I had a good settlement and allowance from the family to keep quiet, so we were able to move away easily."

"But why didn't he come after us when his parents died?"

"It's complicated. He had gotten married, twice, actually, and had just married Irene when his mother died. Plus, you were grown by then." She paused and looked at him. When he didn't react, she continued. Of course, he didn't see all this, but I did. "Additionally, he was in charge of the entire estate and company. He had a lot of responsibility. He checked in on us from time to time, but he was careful to keep his distance."

I personally thought it was a crazy story, but not the craziest I've heard. People do almost anything when money or love is involved, and this had both.

"Why are you telling me this now?"

"You're the heir to his fortune and need to come forward to claim the money."

"And if I don't?"

"Why wouldn't you?" I asked because I was honestly curious. Why didn't I have a wealthy relative leave me a ton of dough? Not that I necessarily needed it, but it sure would be nice.

"I don't need his money. I don't even know him."

Hedy looked at him for a moment. Her face had fallen a bit.

"I guess I just thought you would want to claim your birthright. You're his only child, and if not you, then some awful people stand to get it. They might be the ones that killed us."

"Well, that is different. I don't need the money, but I do want justice for you if you were, in fact, murdered." He looked over at Al and said, "Let's get a few men on this. Have Hacker start digging online?"

Al nodded and started to walk away.

"Oh, wait, Al. Get Catfish too. He's one of the best at this type of thing." Hank looked at me. "Sorry, I gotta pull him from Security, but I'll have Eddie send another guy."

"So, is that it?" Hedy asked me. "Is the reading over?"

"I don't know."

"You don't know what? Did she say something else?" Hank asked.

"She just wants to know if the reading is done. Are you finished?"

"Well, no, but I need to get my men started. You died a little over a year ago, or maybe almost two years. Time flies. I need them to investigate any leads as they will be cold, so the sooner we get started, the better."

"I'd start with Irene and her kids, Dodge and Vera. I never trusted Irene, and Vera is a chip off the ole block. I'd also check out Oren and Viola Crawford. They are cousins. I never trusted them." Hedy said.

"Anyone else?" Hank asked.

"Perhaps his sister, Faye Crawford-Meyers. She always thought the money should go to her twins."

I knew all the names from the news. One of those families famous for being rich and were all influencers, especially Vera and Dodge. They both had millions of followers on their social media accounts.

A scandal like this would have been tabloid fodder for sure had it ever come out, and if Hank did step forward, it would put his business in the news as well. Not just that of the Crawford family. I understood his hesitation.

He liked his life private and had nearly no online footprint. I had looked him up enough to know what was there would be limited and was mostly about his legal businesses. None of his illegal activities, for obvious reasons.

"So, what's the next steps here, Joanna?" Hank asked me.

"Hedy, do you have anything else to say to Hank?" I listened.

"Hank, I love you so much, and I'm so very proud of you. I will understand if you don't step forward for this inheritance, but it really would mean so very much to your father if you decide to."

"I don't know what I will do with that information just yet." He sighed. "I'm struggling to process all of this and just need some time to think."

"Alright, son. I hope that we can reconnect again soon. I miss you so much."

"I miss you too, mother."

That was it. I said goodbye to Hank and his guys. Hedy stayed behind for a moment, saying she wanted to be near him for a while. I walked away feeling good that I could finally give Hank what he wanted most, his mother.

Chapter Six

~ Joanna ~

Now with revenge on his mind, I'm sure that Hank would be able to find the killer, and I wouldn't have to be involved in this investigation. As long as the Crawford family didn't come knocking for more readings, I should be in the clear.

Today was a day off for me, and I didn't have big plans, just a typical Saturday of cleaning, playing with my daughter, and maybe a few errands.

I was about to get Oakley up for the day when I got a visitor that I wasn't expecting.

"Hello." A male voice called out.

"Oh, Senator Crawford, hi."

"Please, call me Arnie."

I had been doing that in my head, but it seemed disrespectful to call him that to his face and not Senator.

"Alright, Arnie. How can I help you today?"

"Hedy told me you went to talk to Hank the other day, and he didn't take the news well."

"That's true. He wasn't happy, but I think it likely just caught him off guard."

"I was hoping that you could do a reading between him and me. Is that possible?"

I wanted to say anything is possible, but I honestly didn't know if I wanted to be involved in this, even if I was the only one who could. Hank got the news he needed and would take it from there. He warned me this could get dangerous and that he didn't want me in harm's way again.

"I don't know."

"Please, I didn't get to be there for nearly his entire life. I really want to explain myself."

"I hope you don't mind me being a bit blunt here, just for my understanding and to help you." I paused because I hated to seem rude. "If you loved Hedy and loved your son, why didn't you tell your family? Why hide it and not claim him from the beginning?"

He sighed. "It's complicated and my biggest regret." He paced and then stopped to look at me again. "This will make me look like an ass, but it's money. If I didn't walk away, they were going to keep everything. Granted, I know some of that money I didn't necessarily deserve, but I had already been working for the family business for ten years when Hank was born. I should have gotten at least the part I earned and the businesses that I started, but because of how the family had everything structured, it was all lumped together."

"Couldn't you have started over?"

"Maybe. I don't know. It felt like I didn't have a choice at the time, but now being 70 years old and dead, it seems absolutely ridiculous that I didn't stand up for them." He sighed. "I wish I could go back to that day, to that moment when I picked my parents and money over Hedy and Hank. I loved them."

"I'm sorry to hear. It must have been lonely."

"It was, but I made time to see Hedy and Arnie... er... Hank for a while. And you know Hedy continued to work for us and lived on the property, so I got to see Hank for a few years. It was strange, and as he got a bit older, he started asking questions and looking like me, so my family started putting pressure on them to leave. They even made some death threats."

"Death threats against a child? That's insane."

"Yes, well, him and Hedy both. All to keep us as scandal-free as possible. They would be so embarrassed by what the Crawford family of today looks like. My father and mother passed before the internet really exploded with all the social media and viral videos. They thought the paparazzi was bad. Could you imagine if they saw how fast gossip travels now?"

"Yeah, it's crazy."

"And Vera, you know my stepdaughter, she is on social media all day, every day. She live streams nearly her whole life. My parents would not understand or approve of that."

"I have seen some of her stuff, so I can imagine."

"Oren and Viola are a bit older than Hank is, so they may not really remember that little kid and definitely had been kept from the details of who he was. Faye was young as well. Father and mother sheltered her in many ways. Then, of course, Irene wasn't part of the family at that point either. This is why everyone felt so blindsided by the terms of my will."

"Understandable. So, do you have any idea who could have murdered you?"

"I'm not sure who could have killed me. They wouldn't have known the details of my will until after. Knowing may or may not have helped their cause, but I guess whoever thought they would be the one to take control. I just don't know who believed it. As my grandfather and father ordered, I would have named that person in my will, and I hadn't named anyone. As I mentioned, I changed the terms to Hank."

"No other reasons at all? Problems with Irene or your sister or your cousins?" They were all people he had named that it could be.

"Well, Irene and I were having trouble. She was sleeping around with just about anyone she could, which I'm sure you've heard. It's not a big secret." He stopped. "I'd started talking to my lawyer about a divorce. She wasn't happy because she would lose her lifestyle if we divorced."

"Wouldn't she get half in a divorce?"

"No, we had a prenup, and it stated a set amount. It was barely a fraction of what she could spend in a year, but it should have been enough to live on until she got a job or found her next sugar daddy. I'm sure you know she is much younger than me."

I nodded. It was at least a 30-year age gap between them. It had been part of tabloid gossip when they started dating. The paparazzi stalked them, trying to get the best pictures, that money shot.

He continued. "Irene and I had a marriage of... convenience, I guess you could say. It was mostly a business deal."

"A business deal?"

"Yes. So, this will make me come off as even more of an ass, but I wanted a young, trophy wife that could keep up with the obligations that come along with being my wife. She had... experience with that. Her first husband was also much older than her, and when he passed, she was looking for her next meal ticket."

"Wow."

"Yes, she isn't completely desolate. She has some money from him, so I had her sign a prenup. I knew who she was. A gold digger. I wrote in a nice... let's call it a payoff to her upon my death. She should be fine, though she may have to work. And as I said though, the amount was less if we divorced."

I was nearly speechless. His tone was harsh and sharp. It was evident that there was no love between them, but the public image of them sure said something differently.

"Well, what about your sister and your cousins? What motive would they have had?"

"As I said, the structure of our family wealth is strange. As the oldest son, my parents left me in charge of the fortune. All the heirs get an allowance from the estate. The way it should have worked is upon my death, it would go to the next heir, Faye, though if I felt she wasn't ready or that someone else in the family was better suited, I could change it. So instead of naming a known heir, as I said, I had it changed to Hank. Then if he didn't claim it, the estate would be divided. There was no reason for it to stay under one person. But, of course, nobody would know that, so Faye may have wanted control."

"That makes sense as a motive. The argument could be made, she got tired of waiting."

"Yes, she wanted to control it, so her deadbeat twin boys could get more allowance each month. We had started arguing about their amount when they turned 18, just months before my death. They are now 20 and should be in college or working, but they follow their mother like shadows. It's weird."

"What about her other kids? Wouldn't they get money too?"

"Yes, but she mostly worries about these two boys. The other two have good jobs and more or less support themselves. They are not a typical Crawford at this point. Paparazzi doesn't stalk them, and they stay out of the limelight. Living normal lives."

"Okay, then what about your cousins? I have met them, by the way. They came in for a reading."

"They did? They're a strange pair. If you didn't know, you would almost think they were a married couple. Always together." He chuckled. "So, who was here from the spirit world to do the reading with? Or were you not able to do one?"

"Oh, I did it, thanks to the fast-thinking Hedy. She pretended to be your mother, Tootie."

"Ha, did she? I bet she did a wonderful job."

"She did." I gave him the story of how it went down.

"Darn, I wish I would have seen that. I bet they were beside themselves."

"They were a little thrown." We laughed. "But, just being strange isn't a motive."

"That's true. I think they thought like Faye was. They wanted to control the fortune to have more allowance from the estate. But I don't know why they would think Faye wouldn't get it, or maybe they thought she would give them more. I don't know, but it was all money for them. All of them."

"Alright, so what about the day of your death? I know not everyone remembers, but weren't there security cameras in your house? Something that would catch something."

"Honestly, I don't know much. I didn't stay to listen in. But since nothing came from it, I assume there wasn't footage, or if there was, it went missing. After all, Irene was sleeping with the head of security, so I wouldn't be surprised if she bribed him to do something."

"Yikes, okay. What do you remember leading up to and then maybe right after your death?"

"Well, let's see. I was having my afternoon cocktail, then I vaguely remember someone coming in. I didn't see who, but I don't think I knew them, or maybe I did. I honestly can't remember. Then everything was blurry, then at some point, I became aware of what was going on. My body was in the sunroom, and the EMTs tried to revive me." He paused, grimacing. "My stepson and stepdaughter were there screaming. All I could think was they were putting on quite a show. I knew they hated me, so they were likely happy I was gone. I left shortly after. I didn't want to hear anything my wife or those brats had to say about me."

"That must have been tough. Do you know what they said was the cause of death?"

"Honestly, I haven't bothered to find out."

"Then why do you think you were murdered. Couldn't you have just had a heart attack? If I remember correctly, that's what they reported as the cause of death."

"I mean, I guess that's possible, but I had a physical recently, and my doctor had given me a clean bill of health. His exact words were fit as a fiddle."

"Were you taking any medicines?" He had to have had something wrong. I couldn't believe at his age that there wasn't something.

"None, like I said, perfect health. Well, almost perfect. Doc said to ease off the alcohol a bit, but nothing too bad."

"Okay, so, did they do an autopsy on you?"

"I don't know. I didn't stick around my family long enough to find out."

"Where did you go?"

"I just wandered around. Nowhere really."

My heart hurt for him. He'd had so much, though I guess what he had was mostly dollars in a bank. He sounded as though he'd lead a lonely, sad life, even with his admittedly selfish moments. I wanted to hug him, but all I could offer was help to tell his story and find the truth about his death. Perhaps, also, helping reconnect with his son.

"I might have a connection that can check for an autopsy."

He looked at me with a weak smile. "That would be great."

"No promises though since you died in Centerville, but it doesn't hurt to ask."

That is if I could get Clint to speak to me. We hadn't spoken much since the internal reviews started, and in our last conversation, he sounded frustrated and angry. It left quite an impression, so I hadn't reached out to him much.

Typically, I would send him cute pictures of Oakley or funny memes, but I had cut back on both. Earlier today, I told him that she had taken a couple of unassisted steps. He replied that she was going to wait for him to walk. I didn't want to admit it, but that was probably true.

"I appreciate it." He smiled. "Now, back to my question about helping me speak to Hank, would you?"

I thought about it. There were definitely pros and cons. Hank deserved to know as much about his father as possible, but he didn't seem interested at all and had a bad temper that I didn't want to get near.

If he felt I was sticking my nose in his business, I don't know what he would do. Thus far, he has only made threats and never followed through. Hank seemed to like me for some reason.

"I can try, but he was adamant that he wanted nothing to do with you or the Crawford family."

"He just doesn't have all the information."

"Maybe so, but he can get pretty angry."

"That's the Crawford way." He smiled. "I know I already said, but seriously, my one regret in life is letting my parents, the media, my board of directors, and Irene run my life. I missed his whole life."

"I'm sorry." I sighed. "I'll try to get a meeting with him."

I picked up my phone and sent a message to Al. He replied instantly that Hank was not interested.

I understand, but this is important to Arnie

He replied that he would talk to Hank about it.

Just give me a few days to broach the subject

"Well, alright, I'll come back in a few days." Arnie said.

Chapter Seven

~ Joanna ~

I still hadn't seen much of Clint. He had been busy with the internal review of his cases. And, frankly, he was a bit frustrated with me for causing all those problems for him. I know he is worried about his job, but honestly, he's a good detective.

The only reason I'd solved the few cases that I did was because I had an inside track and a bit of dumb luck. I had no skills, just an unhealthy curiosity, and that led me to ask the right questions.

Though if anyone asked, especially Clint, I would deny lack of skills.

Regardless, I respected him, and he was the one with the real skills. I wish I could explain that to the internal affairs officer, but I knew that wasn't possible.

Since he was on my mind and I missed him, I sent him a text asking about getting together for dinner.

Can't tonight. Tomorrow?

Sure. After work, my house? I'll cook.

Deal

I'd have to wait to ask him about Arnie's death. I didn't know if he'd be able to help, but I did promise him I wouldn't go to anyone else if I was investigating a murder.

There was a knock at the door, and then it opened.

"Hello." It was Janie, my nanny.

"Hey, Janie."

Oakley heard her and squealed. "Ja-ja."

She crawled her way to Janie, pulling up on her leg when she reached her.

"There's my favorite girl." Janie said as she leaned forward to pick her up. "How's my Oakley today?"

I watched the nanny and my daughter as they had a sweet conversation between them. I had truly gotten lucky to find her. She was patient and loving with my daughter, and the best part was that she could travel if I needed her.

"Well, I'm out of here. Bye, my sweet girl." I kissed her head and then headed out.

In the car, I turned on an audiobook I've been listening to. The one thing I was enjoying about commuting to work was getting to listen to books and podcasts. Something I never got to do when my office was in my house.

I had separated my home and work only a few months ago, and it has been the best decision. I used to love my short commute from the bedroom to my home office and had been reluctant to change that for years. However, after several issues with kidnappings and break-ins, I decided the two lives should be apart. In addition to the office move, I also moved to a new house in a different neighborhood.

"Best decision ever."

I pulled up at work and took in the dark gray stucco exterior of the office complex with its blue glass windows and neat bushes lining the front. The property management company, owned by Hank, had recently added some yellow, orange, and red snapdragons in the landscaping. They were such happy-looking little flowers. Seeing them put a smile on my face and a spring in my step as I grabbed my purse and headed inside.

"Good morning, Tessa." I chirped as I went in the front door. "Oh, good morning, Percy, I thought you were working on something for Hank."

Percy was our security guard and worked for Hank. In my lease agreement, a security guard was to be provided. It was something that Hank had insisted on.

"Good mornin', Ms. Joanna. I was. I am, but today I'm yours." Percy said with a bright smile and a wink.

I nodded, so glad he was here. I didn't like the kid that was sent to replace him. Though to be fair, he was a nice guy, just young and inexperienced. Percy was a seasoned veteran.

He was a handsome older man. His dark eyes always sparkling, and he was quick with his dazzling smile. I couldn't picture him being a hired gun for the town's mob boss, but that's what he did before transferring to the security department.

From Eddie, I had heard some stories about Percy, or Catfish, as the guys all called him because he couldn't grow a full mustache. He had the appearance of catfish whiskers, though he liked to joke the reason was something dirty.

His reputation made him someone I wouldn't want to tangle with, and I was thankful he was on my side.

"Any messages?" I asked Tessa.

"I emailed them to you, but nothing major." She said. "And I printed out your schedule. It's in the usual spot."

"Thank you. You're a huge help as always."

She smiled.

I headed to the back. First stop would be coffee. As I made my way through the hall, I greeted a few of the ghosts that were hanging around. Of course, there were always spirits around. I was thankful they mainly were hanging out here now instead of my house. I used to have a house full almost all the time. Lack of privacy had been an issue, but I asked them to avoid the bedroom and bathroom.

"Oh, hey, boss," Micah said, coming from the storeroom as I was walking by.

"Good morning. How are the wedding plans going?"

"Slow!" He groaned. "I thought it would be easy, but we can't even settle on a date. How will we ever decide everything else?" He laughed.

"I'm sure you'll figure it out." I said as we reached the break room.

I made a beeline for my favorite coffee mug. It had watercolor-style flowers painted on it, which always made me smile. I added one sweetener and a splash of hazelnut creamer.

"I sent you the product order for your approval," Micah said as he filled up his mug. It had a picture of him and Josh on it. So sweet. They were definitely relationship goals.

"Great. I'm going to check emails now. I'll let you know if I have questions."

"Sounds good."

I turned towards my office, but as I got close, a figure going through items on my desk stopped me in my tracks. I knew the voluptuous red-haired woman was not a spirit because her hands were actually touching things. However, I couldn't see her face at all, and as Tessa hadn't mentioned a guest in my office, I had no idea who she was.

"Micah?" I whispered and walked towards his office. "Who is that in my office?"

His eye twitched as if he was as surprised by the news as me. We walked over and peeked through the window. Her face was still turned away from us.

"I have no idea."

"Can you ask Tessa? And alert Percy." I took a deep breath. "I'm going to find out who she is."

Micah's tall strides took him quickly to the reception area while I turned towards the strange woman in my office.

"Hello? May I help you with something?" I said in my firmest tone.

"Well, I take it you are this medium woman." She planted herself in my chair and gestured for me to sit in one of the guest chairs. "It's about time you arrive. I have been waiting for nearly forever."

"Um, I'm sorry. Who are you?" I asked, confused as I sat as instructed. Why was I listening to this stranger? The answer was simply because her tone reminded me of my sixth-grade English teacher, and you didn't cross Ms. MacGregor.

"Why, darlin', I'm Irene Crawford."

"The Senator's wife?" She looked different than the pictures I had seen. She had a new hairstyle or maybe plastic surgery. I couldn't put my finger on it.

"Yes, that's the one." She purred.

At that point, Tessa, Micah, and Percy walked in. Irene stared them down but said nothing. Their eyes went wide, and they slowly backed out of the room, even Percy.

This woman had a superpower that I wanted to learn. She oozed intimidation and exuded power. It's been said that I am charming and can talk my way into or out of any situation, but it was a different skill than Irene Crawford had.

I turned back to Irene, almost scared to speak to her. "What can I do for you, Mrs. Crawford?"

"First, call me Irene. Second, I wanted to get an appointment with you, but the Gothic girl behind the desk said you were booked for weeks. I simply do not have weeks."

I wanted to correct her about Tessa, but honestly, after having so many people mention it, I just go with it now. Tessa had her own unique style that you either loved or hated. Personally, I loved it.

"Well, I'm quite busy and have an appointment soon, so I can't do a reading for you today. Plus, it takes time to prep and channel spirit."

"I don't understand why you can't just do it now. That woman on television does it at the salon or walking through the mall. You're here in your cozy office and can't just... do it." She eyed me. "Are you a fake then?"

"No, I'm very real, but it does take time, and your loved ones are often following you around, or at least that's been my experience." I looked around the room. I had a few ghosts here, but nobody stepped forward for her. In fact, many of them shook their head and left the room. That was strange. Her power of intimidation even worked on the dead. "I don't see anyone here saying they are here for you. I can't do a reading without a ghost."

She stood up quickly and with a loud huff. "Well, this was a colossal waste of time."

I stood as well, trying to match her energy. I wanted to appear as confident and as strong as she did.

"I am very sorry. However, if you want to make an appointment in the future, we can try again." I said forcefully, but my voice shook a bit.

"Medium, I do not have that kind of time. I need answers now." She stomped her cherry red stiletto, but the carpet muffled the sound. "It is a matter of urgency that someone like you could not possibly understand. My whole life is in jeopardy, and you don't seem to care." She spat out.

"If someone has threatened you, wouldn't it be better to go to the police?"

"It's not like that. Someone is trying to steal my money; my lifestyle is at risk. I am a woman who is used to certain comforts, and I cannot have that taken away from me." She flipped her hair and pushed past me.

I stared at her back as she departed. I didn't know how she got in and didn't get to ask her any of the questions I had for her, but I knew Irene was a woman I didn't want to mess with.

Tessa came running back after Irene marched through the reception area.

"Was that Irene Crawford?"

"Yes, it's probably about time I tell everyone what is going on."

With another Crawford coming to speak to me, I decided I couldn't keep this completely to myself.

We locked the front door with a note that said staff meeting. Then the four of us headed to the breakroom.

"Okay, so you've probably noticed the invasion of Crawfords, yeah?" I cringed.

"Yeah, boss, what's up with that?" Micah asked.

"Senator Arnie Crawford came to visit me along with Hedy, Hank's mom."

"Oh wow." Micah said.

"Why?" Tessa asked, at the same time.

Percy was silent and stoic. He seemed to be unbothered. I didn't really know his thoughts on what I did. Meaning if he believed in what I did or not. All I knew is Hank gave him a job, and he took that seriously.

"Well, it turns out the Senator is... Hank's father."

"What?" They both blurted. Again, Percy was quietly listening. I thought the mention of his boss would get some reaction.

"Yeah, so that's why the influx of Crawfords here. There is apparently some drama with the Senator's will and the family fortune that they want answers to."

"And it involves Hank, I assume?" Micah said.

"Yep."

"Let me guess, he was murdered and wants you to figure out who?" Tessa rolled her eyes.

"Sort of. He wants me to get Hank to claim his fortune and name as a Crawford. Hank does not want to."

"Dang, why can't I have a rich relative leave me that much money?" Micah laughed. "I don't care who they are, I'll take it."

"Yeah, I said the same." I said.

"I'm good." Tessa said. "Gotta be happy with what you have."

Micah and I looked at each other and shrugged. We were happy, but I wouldn't mind a couple extra dollars in the bank.

"Well, hopefully those are the last of the Crawfords, but just don't be surprised if we get a few more show up."

"Got it, boss." Micah gave a slight salute.

Tessa nodded, and then everyone got back to work.

"That's the part that I needed to know." Percy finally said. "I will keep you safe, Ms. Joanna."

I was lucky they didn't think my stories were crazy, even if I thought this one was. I still couldn't believe I was wrapped up in another investigation. I just hoped this one wouldn't end as dangerously as the others had.

Chapter Eight

~ Clint ~

I was in my office waiting for the verdict of the Internal Affairs. It should be coming in anytime now, or at least the early results. My stomach was in knots thinking this could be my last day as a detective, as a cop.

Part of me wanted to be positive and have a good attitude, but it was difficult. I was on pins and needles, making it difficult to focus or sit still. I paced and sat, stood, then paced and sat again.

Terry knocked on my door. "Hartley, Chief wants us."

He had gotten a lot more serious since the start of this investigation. He used to be a huge jokester, razzing me about this or that, but lately, we weren't speaking much, just in passing or as needed.

I nodded and stood to follow him. All eyes in the bullpen seemed to follow us as we trekked to the boss' office. It felt a bit like we were being marched to the gallows or something equally gruesome.

Terry knocked on the door.

"Come in." The deep voice of our boss boomed. "Ah, Hartley, Walden, have a seat."

We did as instructed and then watched as the Chief finished an email. I sat anxiously waiting for the hammer to drop, trying not to fidget as we waited.

"Alright, look, you two, I know this internal affairs thing has us all on edge, but I wanted to set your minds at ease. Things are looking good with their findings."

I sat forward in my chair.

"Really?" Terry asked hopefully.

"Yes, well, it's still early, but from what I'm hearing, there is nothing they can see you did wrong. This woman just got really lucky or something."

"She's a medium and speaks to the dead, so she has the inside story." Terry offered.

"Humph, I don't know if I believe all that mumbo jumbo, but we need to know whatever she knows." Chief looked at me. "Aren't you dating her?"

"Oh, um, yeah, I am." My stomach tightened at his words. Was that a good thing?

"Good, good. I want you to be close to whatever she is doing, especially if she gets another case. You know what she knows."

"Okay." I choked.

"Is that a problem? You don't sound confident."

"No, not a problem at all." I cleared my throat. "It's just... complicated."

"Well, uncomplicate it." He slapped his palm on the desk for emphasis.

I nodded, and he dismissed us. We walked in silence most of the way back to our offices.

"So, you going to talk to her?" Terry asked.

"I don't think I have a choice at this point, do I? I already have plans to meet her for dinner tonight, so I'll bring it up then."

"You big romantic you." Terry punched my arm.

"Oh, you know me." I returned the jab. It was good to have him joking with me a bit.

We arrived at our offices. He turned into his, leaving me standing alone. I looked out over the bullpen, all the various personnel moving and chatting. The vibe always got me pumped up and ready to do my job.

At the moment, I still didn't have a case because they had taken them all away temporarily while they investigated, but with luck, I'd have a new assignment soon.

While I was standing there thinking, my cell phone rang. I stepped into my office when I saw the name on the display.

"Hey, Freddy, whatcha got for me?"

"Hey, I don't want to say much on the phone, but I think I have what you're looking for."

Freddy Larson was the Medical Examiner over in Centerville. We'd gone to grade school through high school together. Though I wouldn't say we had been friends, we simply ran in different circles. Back in elementary school, we did attend each other's birthday parties a few times, back when it was assumed the whole class would get an invitation.

Over the years, I have called him about cases that cross the lines between Creekview and Centerville, and he has brought me in when needed.

That is why I'm surprised that no autopsy was done for the Senator. Freddy was thorough and by the books. Autopsies would have been expected in such a high-level case but especially in a sudden death like this one.

"Okay. That sounds promising." I said.

"Will you be able to meet me in Appleton?"

"Today?"

"No, give me about a week. I need to gather the information together. I put it in a safe place, but let's just say... I have what you need for this."

"You're the man, Freddy. Thanks."

"Alrighty, I'll give you a shout once I have everything together."

We said goodbye. I sat there wondering what he could have for me. Oh well, I wouldn't know until he called me back.

I shot off a text to Joanna to confirm dinner. No reply. She must be working. I threw my phone on my desk and paced around my office. Then scrolled through some online news stories and basically wasted the next two hours waiting.

Two weeks without something to do besides answer damn questions had me feeling like a caged animal. I started pacing around my tiny office. I thought the Chief was going to give us some news, any news, so I could get out of this limbo state.

"Hey." My lawyer's voice, Mike, said at my door. "Did they call you yet?"

I hadn't been expecting him. So maybe that meant the results were in, and they were waiting for the lawyers to be here to tell us.

"No. Did someone call you?" I asked.

"Yeah. Where's Walden?"

"I'm here," Terry said from behind him.

"Alright. Let's go find out what this is all about." Mike said.

We went into the conference room, where our chief was sitting along with the IA officer and our union representative.

"Have a seat, boys," Chief said. "The investigation has wrapped up, and I'm pleased to say they have found nothing wrong with your cases. It was just luck that this medium was able to find small details that everyone had missed."

"The findings mean that you can continue as detectives, but we want you to do a more thorough job and not dismiss things so quickly." The IA officer instructed.

"Thank you." We both said. Terry added, "We won't let you down."

"You'll start getting cases again immediately," Chief said with a wink.

Several hours later, I was riding the high from the positive results. After being so down for the last few weeks, I was singing along with the radio all the way to Jo's house. I didn't even care who saw me dancing and singing.

Pulling up at her house, I sat looking at her home for a moment. I liked this one better than her last house and was glad that she had decided to separate home and work. It made her job feel safer, especially after several near misses with her life.

"I could picture myself living here with her," I said to myself as I exited the cab of my truck.

I could hear Chewy barking before I even got a chance to knock and then heard Oakley's squeal as Joanna opened the door.

"Where's my girl?" I cooed as Oakley nearly jumped to me.

"Oh, I see where I rank in this." Jo laughed. I leaned over to give her a kiss.

"You're still my number one," I said to Jo as I scratched Chewy's head and bounced Oakley.

Call me old-fashioned if you want, but this was how I pictured my life, at least in a way. Me coming home after work to my wife, baby, and dog. I could smell the spaghetti dinner Joanna had made for us. It was the perfect end to a perfect day.

We walked into her living room, and I set the baby down as I took a seat on the couch. She immediately crawled and then pulled up next to me. She started babbling with words mixed in here and there.

"She's so close to talking and walking, huh?" I said.

"Yes, any day now on both." She sat next to me. "Dinner will be ready shortly."

"Okay, great. I got good news today."

"Oh yeah?"

"Yeah, they have cleared Terry and me. We are keeping our jobs with no punishment. Though they will be looking at our cases closely for a while."

"Oh, Clint, that's wonderful!" She leaped forward to hug me.

I held her tightly. She smelled like baby powder and oregano. A strange combination, but I liked it. It smelled like home. The embrace ended too soon for me.

"So, then I wanted to talk to you about other stuff as well."

"Stuff doesn't sound good." She chuckled lightly and sat back on the couch.

"It's not bad, just like I mentioned before about work and coming to me with any information you may have about murderers."

"Okay." She looked away, avoiding eye contact with me.

"Wait a minute. I know that look. Who is it?"

"I told you about this already, Arnie Crawford and Hedy Hammersley."

"I was hoping since you hadn't mentioned it again that it hadn't gone anywhere."

"Well, not too far, but I have done a reading between Hedy and Hank."

"So, Hank knows now? I thought I told you to come to me."

"I know, but like I told you, I needed to talk to Hank before deciding if this thing had merit and if he wanted to do anything about it." She crossed her arms over her chest. "Plus, Hank has asked me nearly every day for the past year about his mother. I couldn't withhold that from him. He misses her."

"Did you tell him everything? Like how they think they were murdered?"

"I did."

"Crap. That means he is investigating this now." I ran my hands over my face. This woman would be the death of me. "He's going to cause so many problems."

"No, I'm sure he will be discreet," Jo said.

"How discreet was he when Calvin and Lydia Murphy kidnapped you a few months ago? There was a shootout, you got shot, and they were both killed. None of that had been the plan."

"Well, I got closure on Ted's death at least." She sheepishly said.

"Yes, well, I could have done without the blood bath." I said flatly. "Did Hank say anything about it? When did you talk to him?"

"A little over a week ago."

I guess I would have heard something by now if this would blow up on me, right? I don't know. I watched the baby playing as I tried to think of what else to say.

"Wait, what does the Senator have to do with all of this?" I hadn't thought to ask that before as I'd been too distracted by my job stress. It just clicked.

"He is Hank's father. Hank's real name is Arnold Crawford the second."

"Are you kidding me?"

"Nope, it's a crazy story, but that's it. Hank is Arnold Crawford's son and the heir to the Crawford fortune."

"Well, I'll be... so they were killed to keep a secret or for the money or both, I suppose." Crap, was I starting to believe her craziness? "Are you making all of this up?"

"Why is everyone asking me that?" She threw her hands out with a sigh. "Have I not been right about the other cases? Jeremy and Marcus? The Playhouse Killer? And then, of course, Ted?"

"Shit. I don't know what to think." I sat forward. "This is a crazy story. I need more details."

She filled me in on everything she knew so far, from the love affair to their deaths and everything in between.

"So wait, Oren, Viola, and Irene have recently stopped by to see you?"

"Yep, I'm hoping with Hedy's help, I have Oren and Viola sent off happily. Just so long as they don't speak to Irene." She said.

"I don't think they get along."

"Yeah, I think I heard that, so I should be good there."

"What about Irene? Did she seem happy with what you told her?"

"Not at all. I didn't have Hedy or Arnie there to help, so I just told her no."

"I bet that went over well." I rolled my eyes.

"You're right. I doubt I have heard the last of her."

"Any others stop by?"

"Not yet."

"What's the next steps with this, then?" I had no idea where I was going with asking that, but I had to know what she knew, which meant her next moves.

"Honestly, I'm just waiting on Hank. Arnie wants to talk to him, but Hank has said no. He wants nothing to do with him. He's only looking into the possible murders because of his mother."

"Makes sense." I said and then sat back with a sigh. "You think someone has everything, and they are just miserable."

"Yeah, puts things in perspective, huh?" She took my hand, squeezing it.

At that moment, Oakley stood up in the center of the room, laughed, and walked the roughly ten or so baby steps towards us. Talk about putting things in perspective. Life was short but moved fast.

Chapter Nine

~ Joanna ~

Al finally gave me the word that Hank would speak to Arnie, though Al said he was hesitant.

"He isn't in the mood to have his time wasted, so be short and sweet." Al had said on the phone. "His words, not mine."

I drove over nervous about how this would go. I knew Hank had a quick temper and short fuse. And if he was already giving warnings, it was even shorter than usual.

I tried not to think about it and instead focus on the podcast on the radio, but movement behind me caught my eye.

"Seriously?" What was this person's problem? "Go around." I said, mostly to myself. When they didn't get off my tail, I moved to the next lane to get out of their way. They changed lanes as well.

"Crap..." At least I was driving to Leo's. I tried not to panic. I'd been in this position before.

Then the car turned right into the parking lot of the movie theater.

"Ugh, I'm so paranoid." I laughed at myself.

A few moments later, I was parked at Leo's. I was greeted as always with boisterous hugs and cheers, and a vodka cranberry was placed in my hands before I could even turn it down.

I barely caught my breath from the greetings when I was escorted to Hank's table. I slid into the booth and smiled at Hank. He simply frowned.

"Hello, Ms. Joanna, I heard you have been speaking with my supposed father."

"Um, yes, that's right."

"And is he here right now?"

"He is." I gestured to his left.

He nodded but didn't look. He'd looked when it was his mother, even reached out to try to touch her. It spoke volumes about his feelings on Arnold Crawford. I knew that he wasn't going to like this visit, but I would try.

"And what does he have to say for himself?"

"Well, before we get to that, just want to remind you like always that I will say what he says."

"I got it, Medium." Hank spat out. "Now, what does he have to say for himself?"

Point taken, but while I do this daily, not everyone does, and I liked to spell out the process, even if we had just done this recently.

"I loved you, Junior. That's what I used to call you. You were the cutest little guy. Always following me around."

Hank scoffed.

"Son, I'm sorry. My biggest regret in life is not standing up for you and your mother."

"You didn't even try, at least, from what I hear."

"I did try, but it was complicated."

"Ha, complicated." Hank scoffed. "Fine, but what could you possibly want with me now?"

"It isn't what I want exactly. It's about my inheritance. It's yours. You just have to come forward and claim it."

"I don't need your money. I own more property and businesses in this town than any other person. My wealth might not be Crawford level, but it's more than enough for me." He snarled. "Plus, I know who my children are."

Hank had a few children, all from different mothers. Sadly, the Playhouse Killer had killed one of his daughters. It was the first time I'd learned personal things about Hank.

Of course, I didn't point out to Hank now that he hadn't known about Laura initially. He had a fling with her mother and only learned he had a daughter once she was a teenager. But, of course, he had been a loving, attentive father to her once he found out, so maybe best keep that to myself.

"But I don't want the others to get it. They didn't work for it and don't deserve one cent of it."

"Well, that's not my problem," Hank said.

"It should be. I worked hard for that money, and it should go to my son."

"I'm not your son. There, problem solved."

"This isn't getting us anywhere." Arnie said. "If you don't want it, you don't have to take it, but can you at least claim it? I don't want it to go to Irene, her rotten kids, or my cousins. Donate it all or burn it; just don't let them have it."

"Why shouldn't I let them have it? Give me one good reason."

"One of them, or maybe more than one, killed your mother and me."

Hank stared for a moment. That had gotten his attention. But, of course, I knew better than to say anything that might upset him, and Arnie wasn't saying anything, so I just waited.

"Okay, well, I'm already looking back into mother's death. I suppose I could look into yours too, but not because I want to help you or claim this money, but for my mother. Only for her." He pointed a finger into thin air in the general direction that I had said Arnie was standing.

"I will tell you that I have discussed this with Clint too. He's first looking to see what the autopsy said for Arnie, and then he will look into what his department reported on Hedy."

"You talked to Hartley about this?" Hank snapped.

"Yes, I... I had to. He is, or I guess was, being reviewed at work, like they were doing an internal affairs something. I don't know. I just know he got in trouble at work, and it's my fault."

"If he would have done a better job on Renee's case, then maybe Jeremy and that other kid wouldn't have been dead. Then the serial killer one, had he done his job faster, my beautiful Laura might still be alive along with Macy and many others." He drummed his fingers on the table. "But I suppose it makes sense to have him looking. Fine, I'll give him a call so we can join forces."

"And what can I do?" I asked.

"Stay out of trouble. Keep that precious daughter of yours safe and leave the dirty work to me and the Detective."

"Happy to, but you can't get information from your parents. So, you'll at least need me for that part, right?"

"First of all, that man is not one of my parents, but yes, you're right. We'll need your help. Just stay out of trouble."

"Arnie, any other words for Hank?" I asked.

"Only asking if he thinks he can ever forgive me?" I hesitated to pass on this message, but I did.

"Forgive you? Forgive you?" His voice boomed, and all around the room, pool sticks dropped, and a glass broke when his men dropped everything and anything they were holding, ready to fight for their boss. "How can you ask me that? No, I can't forgive you. Not today and probably not ever. You weren't there for me or my mother. You picked wealth over us."

"No, it wasn't..." But before I could give the rest of Arnie's reply, Hank signaled for Al to remove me.

"Sorry, Ms. Joanna, it's not you, but I can't hear any more of his lies. I will be in touch." Hank said as Al stepped towards me.

Out in the parking lot, Al apologized, but this wasn't the first time I've been kicked out of Leo's after a meeting with Hank. If things kept up like they did, it was likely not the last time either. I thanked Al and told him to give my love to his mother and sisters.

"I sure will, and I'm sure mom would love to have a visit from you soon. It's been a while." Al said before doing his trademark two-finger salute and heading back inside.

"Well, Arnie, I'm sorry you didn't get the result you wanted, but Hank is a tough nut to crack."

"He's definitely a Crawford. Stubborn, holds a grudge, but he'll come around. I just know it."

He thanked me for my time and then walked off. Unlike last time, I couldn't rearrange this whole day, and since I had appointments, I had to rush back to the office.

As I drove back to my office, I thought about Hank and his reaction to his father. I think I would be that angry, too, if my father abandoned me for money. But it wouldn't matter what he said to try to justify it; I know I wouldn't be able to forgive him either.

On the flip side, Hedy should have, could have said something to Hank while she was still alive, anything to soften the blow. She must have known it would come out at some point. Though I suppose it doesn't matter now, she's dead and doesn't really have to deal with the consequences.

Since regaining my power last year, the stories I heard of regret amazed me. It had me thinking about what I might regret in life. I saw daily how short life was, or at least through the words of others, so I did try to not live with regrets.

I tried my best to tell everyone in my life that I loved them. Maybe not my mother, at least not as much as I should. She could be frustrating to deal with, but I did love her. So, I'd make it a point to call her this evening.

My only other regret could be with Clint. Our relationship hadn't grown much from my point of view. We didn't talk future, only the present, and that worked at first, but I think it was time we figured out where we wanted this to go.

I was hesitant to bring it up with him because while I had closure from my first marriage, I knew he still harbored feelings for his lost love.

I sighed as I parked in front of my office. I wasn't going to get anywhere talking to myself. I'd need to speak with Clint.

But for now, I knew that overall, I had very few regrets in my life, which was a really good thing.

Chapter Ten

~ Clint ~

I had a rare day off from work, though it didn't feel like a day off since I would be meeting with Freddy Larson, the Medical Examiner. He finally called to let me know he had the information ready for me.

We agreed on a bar in Appleton since it was neutral ground. It wasn't tourist season, so it should be quiet there, and hopefully, private enough we could talk. But whatever it was he had, it had him a bit spooked. I couldn't wait to find out what it was.

I pulled into the lot with a few minutes to spare. As I'd expected, it was nearly empty. Too early for an evening crowd, too late for lunch. It was the perfect time to meet.

I stepped into the dimly lit bar, letting my eyes adjust before scanning the room for the familiar round face of my old classmate. A hand went up at the end of the bar. I nodded my greeting and headed to this new version of Freddy.

He'd always been a heavy guy with acne and oily hair. However, now he was clear-skinned with styled hair and a trim, runner's body.

"Hey, Freddy. I didn't recognize you for a moment. Lookin' fit." I said, plopping down on the barstool next to him and offering my hand in greeting.

He shook it. "Yeah, I had a health scare a year ago, and it was a huge wake-up call." He gestured down his body. "Now, I have to fight the ladies off, but not too hard."

I chuckled at his joke and then signaled to the bartender for a beer.

"I haven't been here before." I looked around briefly. It was a tourist trap dive bar with an outdoorsy theme. Fishing rods, lobster traps, and mounts of various animals all around. Not my style, but it set a tone.

"Yeah, it's a neat little hole in the wall." He said. "So, how goes things in Creekview?"

"Not bad, about the same."

"I haven't been back in a while, not since my parents moved to Florida."

"You aren't missing much." I chuckled and took a long swig from my beer.

Small talk was difficult, but it was polite, so we spent a few more painful moments chatting about this or that. Nothing substantial but friendly. Old friends catching up.

"Alright, so you asked about Senator Crawford, yeah?" He lowered his voice.

"Yeah? Anything you remember, specifically why there wasn't an autopsy performed?"

"That's the thing." He looked around. "I actually had started it because it's typically expected, and I knew this would be a high-profile case. In fact, I put other cases to the side to focus on this one."

"Oh, yeah?" Of course, he had. Freddy was one of the good ones.

"Yeah, and when I was told the family didn't want it, it seemed odd to me." He then pulled a USB drive from his pocket and slid it to me. "I hid the results and said I hadn't started yet, just prepped him, nothing else. So, I called in every favor I had to keep this quiet and off the books."

"This is everything?"

"Yep, tox report shows scopolamine, and along with the alcohol he was drinking, well, you and I both know that can be deadly, especially at the levels I saw in his system. But I also saw spikes in other things that have me thinking another drug or two might have been used as well." He tapped the drive I hadn't picked up yet. "It's all in there. You'll see."

"Thanks." I picked up the USB and put it in my shirt pocket. "Anything else seem odd that you remember?"

"The family, specifically his wife, seemed very concerned that nothing gets out about his death. The how part of it, that is. She said it would be bad for his reputation." He shrugged.

"Weird. I mean, if it was supposedly a heart attack as reported, why couldn't that leak?"

"The only thing I could think at the time was it was either suicide, and she didn't want people to know, or someone had him killed. You don't have this much devil's breath in your system unless it is one of those two things, and typically the latter. Plus, like I said, a possible second drug."

I nodded. We hadn't had a lot of scopolamine found in Creekview, but what we had was all related to murder or at least had devious intentions when we did.

"So, why are you asking about all this now? It's an old case, or at least out of people's minds. Is the family asking about it?"

I hesitated because people always had an odd reaction to Joanna.

Some were die-hard believers, and nothing I said would change their mind that her powers were just smoke and mirrors. Then you had the other side that didn't and couldn't believe her voodoo.

I sighed. "This is going to sound crazy, but bear with me. My girlfriend is Joanna Webber."

"Ah, the medium with a heart. I love her!" He beamed. "I've seen her do a group reading out in Centerville before."

I'm only moderately surprised that he was a fan. Of course, she was a semi-celebrity and had a lot of fans. But this was a forensic scientist, and shouldn't he be ruled by facts and logic?

"Well, then you know what she does, and she says that Arnold Crawford has spoken to her and said he was murdered."

"Shit, man, I'm glad I kept this then." He chuckled. "Didn't she help you on a few other cases before? I thought I heard chatter about that."

"Yeah, yeah. She seems to have been right a few times, so I like to check out her leads and see if anything comes from it."

Not a complete lie, but I didn't need to tell him that my job was on the line if I didn't know what she knows. Though nobody was looking at this case and it was never one I worked, but still, I had something to prove to myself.

"Dang, I would be hitching my wagon to her and running all of my cases by her before reporting them out. She can get the real scoop for you."

"Yeah." I half-laughed. I didn't know how I felt about that, but the longer I knew her and the more I heard, even I had to admit, it might have merit.

"Let me know if you need anything else, but I have gotta be gettin' back." Then, he signaled for his check. "I'm definitely interested in how this pans out."

"I'll let you know."

We both settled our tabs and then parted ways at the parking lot. I wasn't quite ready to head back to Creekview, so I decided instead that a long hike through the nature preserve with some fresh air and exercise would help clear my head.

I drove from the bar the few miles down to the park entrance. With it being off-season, it was empty, and they waved the standard entry fee. I parked in the lot near the visitor center. From here, you can access all the various trails.

I would try not to think about the last time I was here when the Playhouse Killer had kidnapped Joanna. She had been found safe, and that's all that matters. Plus, she wasn't found in this part of the park.

It was a gorgeous, clear day but cool. I stretched as I studied the park map, trying to decide which path to take. Finally, I decided on the two-miler that would take me around the lake. It was a shorter one but perfect to clear the head.

In the summer months, you would see turtles and alligators basking in the sun, but there were none today. There would also be families or lone hikers, some with dogs, but again, everything was quiet and still. As I walked, I didn't pass a soul.

My only company were the few birds chirping and flitting around in the trees, and the occasional squirrel that would run out on the path, stop to look at me, and then scurry up a nearby tree. Most of the foliage was brown and in hibernation for winter.

I thought about what Freddy said about Irene's insistence that things be quiet and her rush to cremate without an autopsy. That seemed suspicious. I couldn't wait to dig into this drive, and then I might want to look at what her alibi was for that day.

I didn't have any buddies over at the Centerville Police Department, but maybe I could ask Terry if he knew someone. Or I could call my Uncle Doug. He was the chief up in Redlynne and might know people at Centerville.

I shook my head. I didn't need to bring more people into this. At least, until I looked at the information Freddy gave me or found other clues, there was nothing much I could do.

"I don't want to think about this case right now," I mumbled.

Instead, I would focus on my walk and the beautiful nature around me. I stopped on the path to watch a few ducks swimming around the lake. Taking a few breaths to clear my head, then I pushed on down the trail.

I took my time and then decided to loop around once more around the lake to make a four-mile trek. Though the second time I went a bit faster to get the heart pumping a bit.

When I reached my truck a few hours later, I felt a lot more clear-headed and relaxed. I headed home to see what was on this drive and to see if what Freddy claimed was a possible murder was, in fact, that.

Chapter Eleven

~ Joanna ~

Now that Oakley was walking, there was no stopping her, and I had to babyproof differently. With each stage, I had to redecorate and rearrange the house to keep things out of her hands and keep her safe. I know Audrey used to talk about that when her boys were small, but I didn't get it. I do now.

Audrey had taken Oakley for me so I could do some chores and the babyproofing. She loved having her niece as much as Oakley enjoyed being there with her. Also, it was good for Oakley to spend time with her cousins, Harris and Dylan.

I had just gotten some of my knick-knacks rearranged when my phone rang. The display said Clint.

"Hey, Clint."

"Hey, are you busy?"

"Just doing some cleaning and babyproofing, especially with little miss on the move like she is."

"I need to come see her again soon."

"She's with Audrey right now, or I would invite you over."

"Ah, no problem." He chuckled. "I was actually calling to let you know about the autopsy for Senator Crawford."

"Oh, you got the results back?"

"Sort of the unofficial results. My buddy over in Centerville had started one, but the family called a halt to it, saying they didn't want it done. Freddy lied, saying he hadn't done it, because he thought their reaction was super suspicious. Anyway, it definitely seems like foul play could have been a factor here."

"Yeah, that's weird. If there wasn't something nefarious going on, I would think they would want one. This makes me think they had something to do with it."

"Exactly, but for one, they have money. People don't always question those with money, or at least that's my experience. Secondly, it seemed plausible that a 70-year-old man would drop dead from natural causes, and nobody in the DA's office or any police agencies thought it suspicious enough to check out. So, they just took the report and the family's statement as fact."

"But your friend did the autopsy, so what did it show?" I asked.

"Do you know what scopolamine is?"

"Yes, it's a patch for seasickness, right?"

"Yes, that's one use for it, but it can also be bought as a powder, illegally, and then used to control people. They have no memory of it. In some cases, it can cause death."

"Whoa, and this was in his body?"

"Yes."

"Is that all?"

"No, it looks like there might have been something else in his system because there was a spike in succinic acid and choline, above what the body would normally have."

"I don't even know what that means, but it sounds like something, right?"

"Yes, it means that it could be something like succinylcholine which paralyzes the muscles in the body. Meaning the person stops breathing. It takes a keen eye to notice it in an autopsy, as those two things are normally found in our bodies. Freddy has that special eye for details like this."

"Wow, so what's next?"

"I'll continue to dig into it. When do you get Oakley back?"

"A few hours."

"Want to go to dinner? The three of us." He asked.

I smiled. "Yeah, I would like that."

"Great. I can pick you up first, and we pick her up on the way?"

"Perfect."

"I'll tell you the rest later. Okay?"

"Sounds like a plan."

We hung up, and I continued to sit there staring. This story got wilder and crazier with each piece of the puzzle. It was like the perfect storm to murder. But without the Senator's body for further testing, we had to go with the secret autopsy and limited clues.

After a few minutes of pondering, I couldn't put off the last of my tasks, so I pushed up and got busy.

A few hours later, I was dressed for my date and waiting when there was a knock on the door. I assumed it would be Clint. Chewy ran down the hall barking wildly.

"Okay, let's let Clint in." I patted the dog's head as I opened the door. "Hank? I thought... Hi, what brings you by?"

"I found out some information, just a tiny bit, and I wanted to talk about it with you. And, of course, see if my mother was here by chance." His voice softened as he said, mother.

"Sure. She's not here, but come in." I looked out the door. "Did Al come?"

"No, I'm alone."

That was strange. Hank always had someone drive him. He was serious about whatever he was going to tell me.

"Please have a seat. Would you like a drink?"

"Some water, if it's not too much trouble."

"No trouble. Just give me a moment."

He had never taken me up on my offer of a drink before either. Hank was acting very strange indeed.

I got one of my new frosted highball glasses, added a couple of ice cubes, then filled it with filtered water. I was stalling a bit because I was mildly nervous about this Hank that was in my living room playing with my dog.

He was different. Not as mob boss-like. He was softer and gentler in some ways. He didn't have his ever-present bodyguard slash driver with him. He was being friendly and like a guest, not a business associate and mobster.

I could stall no more, so I picked up the glass, put on my best Joanna, a medium with a heart stage smile, and joined him in the living room.

"Here you are."

"Thank you." He took a sip. Perhaps he was stalling a bit too. "So, I've been looking into my mother's death. We had pulled out all the stops when she died. I had an autopsy, though there wasn't much of a body left after the fire. I wanted to know everything." He played with the condensation on the glass he was holding. "They showed a broken spine and neck. She had been lying at the bottom of her stairs. I had security cameras installed for her, and at the time, we couldn't recover them. Unfortunately, it was an older system that wasn't saved into the cloud or a network, like the newer systems. I kept saying I would upgrade it for her, but she insisted it wasn't necessary."

I nodded. He took another sip of the water and composed himself. His eyes had glassed over as he spoke, and his hands were shaking slightly. I wanted to hug him, but I wasn't sure how he would take that gesture.

"We had an arson investigator go through every bit of the house. Nothing unusual in the sense it wasn't arson. Just the burned pan on the stovetop had clearly been the source. He showed me where the scorch marks were concentrated around the vent hood and cabinets. The house was a total loss between the fire and smoke damage."

"I'm sorry." I reached my hand out and squeezed his.

He looked up with tears in his eyes. Then, he smiled weakly at me as he squeezed my hand back. I think this is the first time we have had such a sentimental, intimate moment.

"Thanks, but I do still think it's possible she was murdered. The fall is the part I was having a tough time with. She might have been 70 years old, but she was still nimble. She still worked out daily and participated in 5Ks. She was a badass, especially for her age." He chuckled. "I've had Hacker going through the hard drive from her security system to see if he could access it with some of the new technology we have now." He paused.

"And?"

I should have asked how he was able to keep the equipment, why it hadn't been taken as evidence of some sort, or what condition the hardware was in, but honestly, none of that surprised me. Hank was resourceful, and when it came to his mother, I saw he would do whatever it took to find answers.

"No, not exactly. He was able to get a few days' worth, but not much. The day he got showed a figure stalking around the outside of her house. I have a few of my guys looking into that. Hacker is still trying to get more data from it. It was heavily damaged, and honestly, at the time, I didn't work hard enough to get any data from it because of the autopsy results, and based on what the arson investigator said, it just seemed like the answer, even though I didn't like it."

"I understand. Death of any kind, expected or unexpected, is a hard pill to swallow. This person you loved is gone forever."

I saw the aftermath of death often. No matter how long it had been since the loss, the grief in people could be raw.

"It really is." He sighed. "Well, Ms. Joanna, have you heard anything new?"

"Actually, I just heard from Clint about the autopsy for Arnie a couple of hours ago."

"I don't care as much about his." He rubbed his chin. "Alright, what did it say?"

He might not admit it, but I could tell he was curious about his father.

"There wasn't one done, at least officially, but unofficially it shows the drug scopolamine. Then possibly a second drug called succinylcholine. Clint said it leaves behind succinic acid and choline, which can be found normally in the body, but that Senator Crawford's were slightly elevated."

After Clint had told me the results, I had to look all of this up online to fully understand it. I still wasn't sure if I completely understood it, mainly how someone got these types of things. I guess I didn't have an evil mind or murder in my heart.

"Wow, scopolamine is a dangerous drug." He paused, looking at me for a long moment. "I'll look into it and get with the detective about this too."

"I don't know if there will be much to look into or find. If someone did kill him, all the physical evidence is gone."

"I know, but there is likely a digital footprint of some sort. Those drugs didn't just appear. And I have the best hacker on the planet. So, if there is something to find, he will." He winked then stood. "I will get out of your hair now. I appreciate your time, and please, if you hear from my mother again, I would love to talk to her. I know it's not in her voice, but I can hear her in here." He patted his chest.

"I will. I promise."

As we reached the door, he turned and took my hands. "Do you believe this Arnie person could be my father? I mean, you can see him. Do I look like him?"

I looked at Hank. I had known him now for about a year and knew of him for much longer. I suppose he was a good-looking older man, and he always had women flocking around him, but he wasn't my taste. He always reminded me of my old science teacher.

His gray hair was slicked back and parted to the side, cut neat and tight on the sides. He was slightly chubby and stood only a few inches taller than me. Each time I saw him, he was well-dressed and had this confidence about him that made him feel like a bigger, larger person.

His eyes showed age, but they still held a spark of life in their deep green color. At times, there was anger there and other times kindness. He was an interesting man, and I had enjoyed getting to know him this past year.

"Honestly, I do see the resemblance in you. I think you should look for pictures of him at your age."

He nodded and turned towards the door. I opened it to find Clint in mid-knock.

"Hello, Detective." Hank said, then pushed past him. "Thank you for the talk, Joanna. And, Hartley, I'll be giving you a call soon."

Clint nodded and watched him walk away, then turned towards me. "What was that about?"

"You know what it was about. His mother."

"And anything else?"

"No, just that he has been trying to piece together her death. Did you know she used to run 5Ks? He said there was an arson investigation and that it showed a kitchen fire and that her autopsy was consistent with a fall down the stairs." I stopped short of the information about the man creeping around her house days before. I wasn't sure if that was relevant.

He eyed me, possibly trying to decide whether or not he would believe me.

"Well, okay." He said. "Ready to go?"

Chapter Twelve

~ Joanna ~

"And, Mr. Carter, did you have any final words for your wife before we wrap up?" I said to my current clients.

"Just that I love you and miss you each and every day."

"I love you too," I said for the wife. She had passed after a long battle with ovarian cancer the year before.

With the reading complete, I walked Mr. Carter out to the lobby. When I got there, I noticed a group waiting. I instantly recognized them as Faye Crawford-Meyers, Arnie's sister, along with her twin sons. But, unlike the other Crawfords I had met, they all looked exactly as they did on the news and online; plastic and shiny.

Were they my next appointment? I had seen the Meyers family on the schedule, but I hadn't connected the dots to it being Faye Crawford-Meyers.

I checked the time to ensure I hadn't run long with my last appointment. Nope, in fact, I was a minute or two early, and I should still have about twenty minutes. I needed to clean up the reading room, I wanted to grab a cup of coffee, and I needed a trip to the ladies' room.

"Tessa, are they my next clients?" I whispered.

She simply nodded.

I stepped over, plastering on my most perfect stage face. "Hi, the Meyers family?"

"Actually, it's Crawford-Meyers. Thank you." She said through clenched teeth and a fake smile.

Faye was about as friendly as Irene but maybe less intimidating. Her eyes didn't look right to my soul the way Irene's had. She had a softer posture yet was still confident.

"I'm sorry." I looked over my shoulder to Tessa, who I could see making a note and she mouthed that she didn't know. "You're a few minutes early. If you will allow me time to recharge after my last reading."

"Fine, but do not take long, darling. My time is extremely valuable, and I was here on time." She huffed in her seat. Her sons barely took their eyes off of their cell phones.

"Thank you. I won't be long, I promise."

I turned and walked to the door separating the lobby from the back offices. I turned once and smiled before disappearing and sprinting to my office.

"Hedy, Arnie, are you anywhere close by? Please, please join me here." I said to my empty office. "Please, please."

I ran from there to the reading room and cleaned up the space, wiping everything down, adding a new box of tissues, changing the trash bags, and bringing in new bottles of water and snacks. I thought the boys might like them. I didn't really know much about late-teen or early twenty-year-old boys, but everything I heard was feed them.

"Hedy. Arnie. I really need you both or at least one of you." I said again.

Next, I ran to the restroom to freshen up. Again, I had to look composed and calm.

"Breathe in, breathe out." I did as my reflection directed. "Okay, you've got this."

Though my heart was pounding, I paced myself as I walked back towards the lobby, whispering for Hedy and Arnie the entire way. This hadn't worked in the past, but a few times, I got lucky, and the right ghost showed at the right time. So please let this be one of those times.

I pushed open the door to the lobby.

"Mrs. Crawford-Meyers, please come this way."

"About time." She snapped as she stood and marched my way. "I considered just leaving." She added as she pushed by me, tossing her high ponytail nearly in my face. The boys close on her heels.

"I'm sorry," I muttered. "This way. The door on the left."

We filed in. The boys plopped in two of the three high-back armchairs, leaving one for either myself or Faye. The other would be stuck with the oversized couch. Not exactly my ideal choice for doing the reading.

With me seated in one of the high-back chairs, I felt it gave off a more professional image while families took the couch and other chairs. Perhaps it didn't matter, but it's just how I had always done things, and I was a creature of habit.

Of course, before I could direct her to the couch, she claimed the other chair. I stifled a curse and sat on the edge of the sofa. I fidgeted to find a professional pose before speaking.

"Welcome. You're hoping to connect with a loved one on the other side." I looked around the room, still hopeful.

"Obviously, why else would I be here?"

"Right. It's just part of my process." I died a little inside. "Before I start, there is water and snacks if you would like either. I have boxes of tissues in case you need it, and at any time if you would like to stop, please let me know."

The boys grabbed up a couple of the snacks and a bottle of water each, then right back to their phones. It was going to be difficult to concentrate with the rustle of the bags and the smacking, crunching sound, but at least I now knew they were human.

"Fine, fine. Can we get on with it?" Faye tapped her foot.

"Okay, let me just..." I closed my eyes and pretended to meditate a bit. A stalling technique I had used back in my faking it days. "Ah, let's see. Are there any loved ones here to speak to the Crawford-Meyers family?"

"I'm here, Joanna. I'm here." My eyes flew open at the sound of Arnie's deep, soothing voice.

Oh, thank goodness, I thought. "Ah, yes, we have Arnold Crawford here. That's your brother, correct?"

"Yes, and just the man I wanted to speak to." Faye perked up, her voice smoothed. "Arnie, darlin', you have left quite a mess behind here."

"Before I start giving his messages to you, I will speak word for word what he says."

"I assumed that's how it worked. Now please tell me what he said." She clapped her hands at me.

That had me leaning back and blinking several times. She was an incredibly impatient person.

"Oh, okay," I stammered. "He asks, has he? What do you mean by a mess?"

"Yes, you have, and you know damn well what I mean." She snapped.

"What did you do to earn that money? Why should I have left it to you?"

"It isn't all yours. Some of that is dad's money, and some is grandpa's. You're just the oldest, so you got control of it. Now you're gone. It should be me." She said, crossing her arms over her chest.

"It's always about control with you. You didn't work the family business; that was me, dad, and grandpa. It was my decision of what to do with it, and it should go to my son."

"You claim he's your son, but who is he? Some random, unnamed person that none of us know. What did he do to deserve our family's money? Nothing."

"He's not random or unnamed. I know him and his name."

"Arnie, you never had children. It could be some gold-digging woman just making this claim. There is no proof." She huffed. "I don't think you were in your right mind when you created this will, and I'm trying to get that proven and your will overturned."

"Not if I have anything to say about it."

"Say about it? You're dead. See, he is clearly not making sense now."

I didn't say what else he said, which frustrated him. I would address him on it later.

He sighed when he realized I wouldn't pass along his message.

"Fine, Ms. Webber, if you won't say that, then just tell her I'm sorry that we didn't have the best relationship growing up, but with our age gap, I was moved on with my life by the time she was born. And I'm sorry that you don't understand why I left my money to my son. Mother and father knew about him and forced him out of my life. It was my biggest regret, and this was my way of fixing it."

"You're sorry? That doesn't resolve this." She huffed. "But, I will have what is owed me and my boys." She snapped her fingers as she stood. "Come on, boys."

They jumped up and followed her out. They never once said a word or acknowledged my presence, other than eating half the snacks I'd laid out, leaving the wrappers strewn around. They followed her like puppies. Weren't they old enough to think and speak for themselves, even have jobs, and not follow mommy all day?

Different strokes, I supposed.

I peeked out the door of the reading room. From here, I could see through the window out into the lobby. She stopped at the reception desk. I hoped to pay, but honestly, I wouldn't lose sleep over it if she just walked out.

"What happened to you, Ms. Webber? Why didn't you say everything?" Arnie asked.

"I can't tell her everything you said because you don't want to give her any information about Hank or Hedy, which could clue her in to him, and if she's the killer, you don't want that, right?"

He groaned. "You're right. She was just pushing all my buttons. We never had much of a relationship, and honestly, my father doted on her and her mother, my stepmother, treated her like a delicate doll. Delicate like a bomb if you ask me."

"I'm sorry." I said. "Family dynamics can be tough. She's impatient, that's for sure."

"Yes, she's just used to getting her way, is all." He said.

"I'm so glad you came by today. Did you hear me, or how did you know to come?"

"I was just coming to check in with you since it's been almost a week since I talked to you last. I thought I would see if anything new had come up."

Bummer. I had really hoped calling out to him had worked. Though it hadn't worked yet, so I shouldn't be that surprised. It was something I'd have to keep working on.

"Well, actually, yes. I found out about your autopsy. It's an unofficial one because your family asked that one not be done."

"Really? That's suspicious, right?"

"Very suspicious, especially with the results. It points to possible murder unless you killed yourself."

"I would never have. Other than being in a loveless marriage that I was looking to end, I was overall happy."

"Well, then someone poisoned you using two different drugs. One is typically used to turn you into a zombie-like state, and the other paralyzes your entire body. After that, it all just stopped functioning."

"Wow... um, wow. That's tough to hear, but okay, so now what?"

"My boyfriend is still looking for leads, and Hank is doing that as well. He has his best men on it."

"Your boyfriend?"

"Oh, yes. He's a detective and the one that got the autopsy."

"Excellent! Happy to have good men on this case." He smiled.

"Yes, so don't give up hope. I won't. Not until we've looked at every possible clue we can, and the fact that your family keeps knocking on my door means we might be on to something. We just have to prove it."

"Well, okay then. I will check back with you in a few days or a week. Thank you so much for all your help."

With that, he was gone, and I was alone trying to process Faye's visit. Irene was intimidating in a businesswoman fashion, one used to running board meetings and delegating tasks and projects. Faye was intimidating in more of a spoiled rich kid all grown-up way. Bossy and used to people bowing to her.

I had to be honest. I didn't know which one I'd rather work with.

"Neither." I said to myself as I cleaned up from the Crawford-Meyers appointment and prepared for my next clients.

Chapter Thirteen

~ Clint ~

I was working in my office, waiting on a case to come my way. In the meantime, I was filling my time looking into Senator Crawford's death. Those drugs had to come from somewhere. So, I was doing some online research to determine the most logical places to find it.

Though I knew it wasn't going to be an online retail store or anything. It would be illegal channels. Possibly black market shipped in from another country. I had a few places I could look, but the best bet was if I could access the computer it was ordered from.

I'd need warrants to search computers and electronics.

"I wonder if Mrs. Crawford still has his phone and computer?" I thought out loud. Doubtful, but it might be worth a shot.

Perhaps one of the other Crawfords, like the siblings Oren and Viola, or his sister, Faye. Then there were Irene's children, Vera and Dodge. They both had a huge online presence. It wasn't that much of a stretch that one of them could have access to these things.

Could they have gotten it for the Senator? That is if we bought in to the theory he did this himself. Or if they got it for their mother?

Had Irene plotted with one or both of her children to take him out?

I'd just need to speak with my boss and then file the paperwork. Of course, he'd think I was crazy. It would be a long shot to prove anything on a nearly two-year-old case. Strike that, two cases, but I had to try if only to prove to myself that I was a good detective.

But he said if Joanna gets wind of another murder, I need to be right there with her. I need to know what she knows. This is what she knows, so I was going to bank on him authorizing the warrants, or at least helping me break down barriers to get it through Centerville.

I pulled up the files on Hedy Hammersley. It's just as Jo had said. The autopsy was consistent with a fall, and the arson investigator ruled out arson. He found no accelerant residue or anything suspicious. I didn't see a toxicology report, but perhaps her body was too charred for one to be completed.

I'd have to go talk to our lab folks, and maybe I could even have Freddy look at these. Maybe he'd see something I wasn't or that our team had missed.

Hank and I kept missing each other on the phone. I wanted to get his thoughts on all this, and he'd said he has information for me as well.

I'd resolve that as soon as I could.

For now, I'd have to figure out how to get warrants without sounding like a nut job.

"Hey, Hartley," I heard the Chief call my name.

"Yeah?" I stuck my head out of my office.

"You and Walden, homicide downtown." He handed me the address. "Don't screw this up." He winked and turned away.

Hot damn! The cold case would have to wait because I had a new one to work.

I gathered my partner, and we both hightailed it out of there. This was our first case since the investigation wrapped up, and we were pumped and ready for it. As usual, Terry drove, and I reviewed the file.

"Looks like a murder-suicide, possibly domestic abuse case." I flipped through the file. "This address has a lot of calls."

"All domestic?"

"Yeah. I can't tell which one was the abuser. It seems like each had as many calls reporting on the other."

The part I hated about this job was the domestic abuse cases. Why did people do that to each other? And when children were involved, it was even worse. Child Welfare Services was on the way to pick up the two young children.

I thought of Oakley's face. She had gotten so lucky to have Joanna adopt her. When she was born, I had been shocked by Cate's request and even more when Joanna agreed. But it had been the perfect match for all of them.

Plus, I couldn't imagine her not being in my life. She had me wrapped around her finger from the first time I got to spend time with her. She was a sweet baby.

"We need to ensure we check everything carefully," Terry said, checking his mirrors and signaling to the left. "I'm so excited to have a case so quickly. Boy, I missed this!"

"Me too."

"So, how are things going with Jo?"

"Okay. About the same."

"What about what Chief told you? Know what she knows?"

"Well, a few weeks ago, she brought up Senator Crawford. Do you know anything about his death?"

"Don't tell me?"

"Yeah, she said he came to her, and also Hedy Hammersley contacted her."

"Hedy's death was worked by Turner and Jackson, I think."

"Yes, I've reviewed the case. From the autopsy, it's consistent with the reported death. A fall down the stairs, and she'd been cooking. The food burned on the stove and caught the kitchen on fire, and it just engulfed the house. It was a total loss."

"That's what I remember too," Terry said.

"She's talked to Hank since it's his mother involved, and get this, Arnold Crawford is apparently his father."

"No way!"

"Yeah. There's no autopsy on him, not officially, and of course, his claim of murder without proof or evidence will be an uphill battle."

"Yeah. For sure." Terry said. "Wait, not officially? Freddy did it, didn't he?"

"Of course. The guy is by the book, and he expected it would be high profile, so he had it nearly complete, all the samples taken, when the family asked for it not to be done. He hid everything thinking it would come in handy someday. Well, that day has come."

"Wow. So, what now?"

"I was looking into the tox report that Freddy pulled. It shows scopolamine and possibly succinylcholine."

"Those are dangerous and not easy to come by."

"Those were my thoughts too, so I was thinking of going after search warrants to see if I could figure it out. I'm not even sure where to start with that, though. Do you think Irene Crawford would still have her husband's computer and cell phone?"

"Maybe. Could be worth looking into, and we should also check hers."

"Yep."

"And what about Jo? I know she lets her curiosity and big heart lead her into danger."

"I told her to bring anything straight to me. No more going off on her own."

"Ha, she's not going to listen."

I stared at his profile, then laughed. "You're probably right, but I can try."

"You gonna marry her?"

"Probably."

I surprised myself with my answer, but it was true. Of course, I had known it for a while now and had started looking at rings, but I kept that last piece of information to myself.

"And, of course, I accept the role of best man."

We laughed and then sobered as we pulled up to the crime scene. A few officers had already gotten the perimeter set up, and one officer was controlling entrance to the area. While others were taking pictures and interviewing witnesses.

The media had already started to set up. Terry would handle them after he spoke with a few of the officers to get the facts. I went to talk to the one who had been interviewing witnesses.

Child Welfare Services had arrived and were taking charge of the children until they could find relatives. The girl was maybe four, and the little boy was barely older than Oakley. It broke my heart hearing them cry for their mother. I wanted to run straight to Joanna's to hug that sweet little girl who I already thought of as mine in so many ways.

"Witnesses said there was shouting from inside the home, and then the fight was moved to the front yard." The officer said, motioning to where the two bodies lay. Thankfully covered with sheets and a barrier set up, so the children didn't see them. "The husband was hitting her and then pushed her to the ground. She pulled out a gun. He got it away from her, shot her. Then he screamed, saying what have I done and then turned the gun on himself."

"Okay." I looked over at the house. The windows were all open. "Were the windows already opened?"

"Yes, that's how people heard them inside."

"Any security cameras either on their house or nearby?"

"We are asking about that now. A few neighbors do and are checking if they captured it."

"Great."

I walked around the scene, careful where I stepped, so I didn't disturb anything. Not much to investigate. We'd talk to a few more witnesses and review video footage, but that was it.

Terry finished with the media and came to join me.

"Sad case. I hate to see this."

"Me too, and seeing those little babies is heartbreaking," I said.

"You know more about that now, huh?"

"Oakley?" I asked.

"Yep. She's got a big piece of your heart, doesn't she?"

"She certainly does." I smiled, thinking of her cherub face and infectious laugh.

A few hours later, we had the neighbors' names who had video footage and had gotten the footage from them. The bodies were taken to the coroner's office, and the site processed and closed out.

I was exhausted, but it felt so good to be working again.

My phone chimed as we climbed into the car to leave. It was Joanna asking if I had dinner plans. I replied that I didn't and instantly received an invite over. I smiled.

"Joanna?" Terry asked.

"Yeah. Asked me over for dinner."

"And you sound so broken up about it." He laughed.

"Ha, yeah. Honestly, I was serious when I said I'm starting to think about a future."

"For real?"

"Yes, sir. I just don't know when yet. It's still a new thought."

"Well, you can't do much better than Joanna. She's a unique and special woman."

"Don't I know it." I smiled and daydreamed on the drive back to the station about my future with my two favorite ladies and that goofy mutt.

Chapter Fourteen

~ Joanna ~

I was five levels deep in an online search of the Crawford family. I'm not even sure what my original search words were, but somehow, I was now watching videos of Vera Beckett, Irene's daughter.

She was good at these viral dances. I tried to imitate one and failed miserably.

"I got my dad's dance skills," I mumbled.

My dad was infamous for being an awful and awkward dancer, but he sure was fun to watch.

After too much time on that, I clicked back to a previous tab where there was an article about Faye Crawford-Meyers. She was getting a divorce from her fifth husband. He was the Meyers. I guess she would be Faye Crawford again soon, and Arnie's argument about having a rich husband would be moot. Though this article did say she would get millions in the divorce, so who knows?

I'm glad I was only semi-famous. Not all of my business was in the news like this. Nobody cared if I did anything because all they wanted was to hear from their loved ones, which was fine by me.

I liked to keep my private life private, and my business was about giving people closure and love. At least most of the time. I did have the occasional bad reading that wasn't perfect, full of anger and fighting, but those were rare.

I clicked from there through an article with a timeline of Faye's previous marriages and relationships. All high-profile, all in the news, all ended badly. She did have children out of marriages two, three, and her two twin sons in number four. None in the first or last.

There were plenty of pictures of all of her children, but the twins were almost like her shadows. They were never far from her. I had witnessed that firsthand.

Her other two children were in their late twenties, and she seemed less than concerned about if they got the money or not.

One was a doctor and looked to be doing well. Recently married and with a baby on the way. The other was a former model and clothing designer in New York. She had just had a big runway show for her designs. They both looked like they were doing well and had only limited mentions in articles about Faye.

Thinking of children had me checking the screen of the baby monitor. Oakley was sleeping peacefully, but her nap would be over soon. I smiled as I watched her sigh in her sleep.

I checked the time. Clint was coming over later. He'd messaged that he had finally gotten to investigate a case and was thrilled. I was happy for him and hoped this would get his career back on track.

"But first a few more searches."

After promising several people that I would stay out of trouble, I was trying to not get too wrapped up in this investigation. But I couldn't help looking, and an internet search in the safety of my home should be okay.

Nobody would know I did it, except for maybe Hacker. He had a reputation for being able to find anything or get anywhere online. I'm glad we were on the same side.

I clicked through images of Irene and Arnie from various moments in their marriage. This one from a gala. Dressed to the nines with Irene dripping with diamonds. Arnie smiling at her, and she looked to be laughing, but there was no shine in their eyes. It was staged for the cameras.

These pictures were shared anytime the Senator made the news. A prominent Senator and his young, gorgeous wife looking so in love. I would never have thought they were faking it, but now having it pointed out, you could see it.

"Wow." I clicked through picture after picture going back years.

A sound on the monitor had me looking up. It was Oakley calling me as she woke up from her nap. Chewy heard her and let out a soft bark.

"You ready to see your girl?" I asked. He wagged his tail as he ran down the hall and then back to me, giving me a sharp bark of impatience. "Sorry, sir, I'm coming."

"Hey, baby girl."

"Ma... ma!"

"Did you sleep well, sweet girl?" I asked as I picked her up and carried her to the changing table.

"Dawg, dawg."

Chewy tried to lick her hand that she had outstretched to him. She giggled, and he wagged his tail. It was like their own secret language.

"You two." I laughed.

They loved each other, and once she was changed, they would play ball or chase until one or both of them tired out.

"Clint will be here soon," I said to her.

"Da."

"Maybe."

After she was ready, I brought her into the living room to play with her best friend. He grabbed his favorite ball and dropped it in front of her. She picked it up then tried stuffing it in his mouth. He gently took it and then ran down the hallway. She chased him giggling the whole time and yelling ball and dawg.

There was a knock at the door. Chewy started barking and spinning. Oakley clapped and yelled da over and over as she toddled to the door.

"Oh, boy," I said as I followed them.

When I opened the door, he said, "Hey. Sounds like I'm just in time for another fun party."

He scooped up Oakley and pet Chewy on the head in almost the same motion and then leaned forward to kiss me.

"Oh, yeah, you know us, always partying." I laughed. "Want a drink?"

"Sure. Beer if you have one."

"Coming right up."

"Thanks." He followed into the living room and stopped there, setting the baby down, and then dropped to the floor. They began playing with the dog.

"Ball." She offered it to Clint.

"Why, thank you." He then threw it down the hall for Chewy to chase. Oakley clapped her hands.

"Ball. Dawg. Ball." She pointed and then ran after him.

"She's really starting to talk." He said as I handed him the beer.

"Yeah, each day a little more." I sat in my favorite armchair. "She is calling you da still."

"Really?" He grinned at her. "Does that bother you?"

"Not really. You?"

He paused and looked at her. She had gotten the ball from the dog and tried to throw it for him. She giggled when it bounced around, and he caught it mid-bounce.

"Honestly, no, I don't mind."

"Then I won't correct her." I leaned over to kiss him. Just a quick, soft kiss on the lips.

We sat watching them in comfortable silence. I knew she really didn't know what da or daddy meant, but she was using it correctly, so that was strange. Perhaps she heard Dylan and Harris call their father daddy, and I also called my dad that. Who knows? She was my first real baby experience.

"So, how was work?" I asked him.

"It was good to be out on a case, but I hate this kind. It was a domestic violence case, and there were young children in the house."

"That's tough."

"It's good to see her." He watched Oakley toddle around with the ball and Chewy following, tail wagging nonstop. "He's such a gentle dog. It's amazing how he just knows she's little."

"I know. I got really lucky with this one." I smiled over at my sweet dog. "I ordered pizza for dinner. I hope that's okay with you."

"Pizza is always an excellent choice."

I hesitated with my next question because I knew he didn't want me involved, but I had to know.

"Anything more about the Crawford case?" I finally asked.

"Not yet. I'm trying to figure out my next steps. My biggest concern is the length of time since he died."

"Yes, that makes it tough. I wish we could have connected with him immediately."

"How would that have helped?"

"Just that we could have investigated it while there was still evidence, like a body and maybe fingerprints, DNA from the murderer, something," I said, unsure if that made sense.

"Have you been investigating this?"

"No, I did an online search of the family just to remind myself about them all, but nothing exciting."

"Okay good, you stay out of this as much as possible. If Senator Crawford was killed, what's to stop someone from coming after you?"

"Yeah, I have had enough of getting kidnapped and held at gunpoint."

"Me too. You've just gotten lucky in the past cases. You don't have skills for this."

That caught my attention and my temper flared slightly. Even if he was right that I didn't have skills, I wasn't going to admit it. Plus, I felt I had at least some skills.

"What? Are you serious?" I scowled. "It wasn't just that I talked to the dead people, you know. With Jeremy's murder, I chased leads. I went searching for clues and evidence."

"Yeah and look what happened to you. Kidnapped and tied up in a warehouse in Buckston."

"True, but it worked out in the end. Cate is behind bars. I have Oakley, and Jeremy and Laney both have closure."

He stared at me with his mouth open.

"What?" I asked innocently.

"Just because that case had a happy ending doesn't mean you should have been involved. And look what happened with Ted's murder. You got shot in the leg."

"Barely, and I recovered from that." Okay, I did get lucky with that one, but again I wasn't going to admit he was right.

"Are you really trying to justify being shot?"

"Okay, fine. It was dangerous, but I'm safe; Oakley is safe. I'm not doing that with this case."

"Good."

"Though I can't help that I keep having Crawfords coming to me or finding me."

"Huh? You've talked to Crawfords other than Arnie?"

Whoops. Me and my big mouth, but I had let the cat out of the bag.

"Yes. Irene, Faye, and Oren and Viola have all come by the office for readings."

"When were you going to tell me that?"

"Uh, now?" I shrugged and flashed my most innocent smile, or at least I hoped that's how it came off.

"Jo, this is important to the case, and I asked you to tell me everything."

"It didn't seem important. I have dozens of people a week that talk to me about their dead relatives. Would you like to know about all of them?"

He shot me a look. "Jo, if your story about Arnold Crawford is true and he suspects one of them killed him, which all signs point to being true, why wouldn't it be important to the case?"

"Okay, point taken, but don't say I don't have skills because I do."

"Fine, babe, you have skills." He said, pulling me down to his side. He kissed my head and then made his way to my lips. "I love you and your awesome skills."

"I love you too."

But that didn't mean I would necessarily stay out of this or tell him everything, as I wasn't sure I was over his little comment about my lack of skills. It just meant I would work hard not to get caught.

Chapter Fifteen

~ Joanna ~

Today, I was heading over to pick up Audrey, and together we were going to find evening gowns for a charity event to benefit Harper's Angels. It was the adoption agency that had helped me with Oakley. They had been so easy to work with, and I wanted to support them in any way I could.

Seats to the event were $3,000 each, or a table for eight was $20,000. So, I bought a table and invited Clint, Micah, Josh, Tessa plus one, and then my sister and her husband, Stan.

Clint said he had a tuxedo. So, with a hot date taken care of, I simply needed a dress, heels, and a fabulous hairdo that Tessa had already volunteered to help me with. She was my stylist for tours, so it made sense.

"I'm so excited!" Audrey squealed in the front seat. "I haven't dressed up like this since my wedding."

"Ha, I haven't worn an evening dress ever, but I did wear that Cinderella-like dress for prom."

"That was a creation."

"Oh yes, lots of ruffles and all that tulle. What was I thinking?"

"Well, I am sure we will find something that our future selves won't regret." She said with a giggle.

"Yeah, I think it's like a little black dress. You can't go wrong with a beautiful gown."

I slid the car into a parking spot in front of Rosie's Glamorous Gowns. It was a newer shop, only a few years old, and this was our first time shopping here.

As I got out of the car, Oakley's car seat in the back seat reminded me how much I missed my girl. Yet, it had perks too.

"It's so much easier having Oakley with Janie," I said. I was able to simply hop out of the car and head in without grabbing her and all her belongings.

"Yes, but just think you'll soon be picking out her prom dress."

"Slow down. Her first fancy dress will be for Micah and Josh's wedding."

"Oh, really? Cute! Have they settled on a date yet?"

"Not yet, but once they do, we will be right back here to find her a lacy little dress."

"I hope you invite me along. I have boys and love getting to shop for girlie things for Oakley."

"I will."

Stepping into the shop, the faint scent of roses and lavender hit me first, causing me to gag slightly, but it quickly passed. There was soothing, soft, smooth jazz music playing, and everything was crisp and white in this immediate area. Clearly, they catered heavily to the bridal crowd.

"Hi, welcome to Rosie's Glamorous Gowns. I'm Bonnie. How may I help you?" Bonnie greeted us before we made it two steps in the door.

"Yes, we're going to the Harper's Angels charity event next month and looking for evening gowns or maybe cocktail dresses. Whatever speaks to us." I said with a laugh.

"Of course, of course. We have a huge selection. If you'll follow me."

She led us through aisles and rows of wedding dresses. I couldn't help but wonder if I would ever wear another and take that walk down the aisle. I sighed.

"Thinking about weddings?" Audrey whispered.

"Yes. It felt like such a fairytale, and it turned out to be... not so much."

"I'm sure your second, and might I add, final one, will be the most magical. I will make sure of it."

"Alright, ladies, here we are. I will let you browse, and I'll get two of our dressing rooms unlocked and ready for you." She smiled and then gestured. "I'll be nearby, so just shout for me. Again, I'm Bonnie."

"Thanks, Bonnie," I said with a smile.

We turned to eye their selection. There seemed to be miles of dresses. It was a bit overwhelming, but when you really looked, it was divided by color and style and then sizes within those.

"What color are you thinking?"

"I think I look best in blues." Audrey said. "Or maybe I just think that because it's my favorite color."

"It does look good on you and makes your eyes pop." She had gotten our fairer genes. The English side of our family. I had darker features and took after our Italian side.

"And for you, I think... maybe wine-colored or a deep, sexy purple."

"Ha, the medium... sexy?" We heard a woman say behind us.

We turned to see Irene Crawford coming out of a dressing room in a drop-dead gorgeous dress with a neckline that went nearly to her navel. It was covered in fire engine red crystals that sparkled as she moved towards us. Not what I would picture a lady her age wearing, but she had the body for it, so good for her.

"Hi, Irene. That dress is stunning on you." I said politely.

"I know." She said, looking over her shoulder at her reflection in one of the many mirrors. She did the pouty lip pose at herself, shifting to check her back at different angles in the mirror. Then turned back to me. "What are you doing here? This doesn't seem like your type of place."

"Well, no, I mean not normally what I would wear, obviously, but we are going to a charity event, and it's formal, so..." I gestured towards the dresses.

"Not Harper's Angels?" She scoffed.

"Yes, actually, that's the one."

"Why? How can you afford that? That little medium gig you have?" She chuckled. "Doubtful."

"Actually, I do quite well at my little gig."

"You don't have to defend yourself to her. Clearly, she doesn't know." Audrey said.

"What don't I know? That she's a fraud? Yes, I do know that. Couldn't even do a reading for me with my... my late husband." She started crying and collapsed into a nearby chair, but I knew it was for show. There weren't even tears, just a lot of acting.

A couple of salespeople came running. One started fanning her, and another had a box of tissues.

"What I said was, he wasn't present that day. Just because we may be ready to speak to the spirit world does not mean they are ready to speak to us."

All the salespeople and a few customers turned to look at me. If looks could kill, I would be dead.

It gave me an idea though, since there were several spirits here, so perhaps one could help me out.

"Alright, let's see," I started. "There are actually several ghosts present now."

All eyes that were once drilling into me started darting wildly around. I listened as many voices started shouting out to me. I tried to focus on one at a time.

"My daughter is here buying a wedding dress. Please, tell her I'm here watching." One lady yelled.

"Who is your daughter?" I asked her. Everyone followed my gaze.

"Ariel Garcia."

"Is there an Ariel Garcia shopping for a wedding dress?"

There was a gasp, and a young woman stepped forward from the back of the crowd that was slowly forming around us. She was wearing a mermaid wedding gown with a lace overlay and sparkled slightly in the light.

"That's me. Is it...? Is it really my mother?"

"Yes, Ariel Angel, I'm here. And I think that second dress you tried on with a bit more bling is more your style." I said, passing the message exactly as she said.

"You couldn't have known about that dress. It has to be my mom. She's the only one that calls me that too." She giggled as tears slipped down her cheeks. "Oh, I'm so glad you are here. This has been so difficult not having you here to help guide me."

Ariel and her entire group hugged each other with tears streaming down their faces.

"I will be right by your side today and every day, including your wedding day. He seems like a wonderful man too."

"Thank you," Ariel whispered.

The salespeople grabbed more tissues and started passing them blindly to anyone who even looked like they might cry.

"Next, is there a Lily here?"

"That's me!" One of the salesladies said.

"Your grandmother is here." I paused to listen. "I'm so proud of you and all you have done for yourself. Getting sober and moving forward. Taking the steps we outlined before I passed."

"Oh gran, thank you. I've tried."

With each reading I did, the crowd turned from Irene's side to my side, and she was soon pouting from the lack of attention.

"Well, so? A few dozen readings don't prove much. You can't do mine." She retorted with a stomp of her foot.

"I'm sorry, Irene, I can only work with the spirits that are present now." I looked around. "These women all had family here today. And I'm sorry that I can't do everyone here. But I really need to get back to my shopping."

The crowd murmured thanks or praise as it broke up, and everyone returned to what they were doing before Irene's hissy fit. That is everyone except Irene. She had to keep pushing my buttons.

"You never said how and why you're going to this thing. What do you care about this group?"

"They are the ones who helped me adopt my daughter." I said firmly. "I believe in their mission."

I turned, trying to end the conversation with her, and tried to focus on the dresses, but I could feel her coming closer to me.

"Oh, that prison baby you adopted from the dead Landon guy and the whore who killed him." She particularly purred out the words as if trying to get my goat. Test how far she could push me before I snapped. Calling Cate a whore did it for me.

"She is not a whore, but yes, yes, that's my daughter, and I would ask that you speak about her with respect. She didn't ask to be born from an affair and get caught up in a horrible love triangle. She's just an innocent, little soul." I was seething.

Audrey put her hand on my shoulder and then took over my rant.

"And that is a young child; you should not speak that way about a child. As my sister said, we will be attending, and she is a celebrity in her own right. Unlike some people, she didn't take the easy way to money." Audrey let her gaze look Irene up and down. "She has worked for every penny she has. She worked long hours and did well for herself. And as you can see, she's not a fake, so I will ask that you get back to your shopping and mind your own business."

Irene looked around to see if she would get backup from anyone else. Everyone was just staring at her, with a few giving her a smirking once-over. She huffed then turned back towards her dressing room.

The room around us was filled with soft claps. Audrey and I smiled at them and then each other before returning to our shopping. Minutes later, a stomping Irene came out of the dressing room.

"I will never shop at this store again," Irene shouted and then made her way to the door.

She paused there to look back. Again, nobody batted an eye, making her huff loudly as she finally pushed out the door.

Bonnie joined us as we selected a couple of dresses. "Thank you for running her off. She's the worst."

"I didn't mean to make a scene, but if it helped, then you're welcome," I said, smiling.

"I'll get this set up in the dressing rooms. You can come over once you're ready to try them on." Bonnie said as she stepped away with the gowns we had selected.

The rest of our experience was wonderful. We got pampered by every salesperson, even getting champagne, which we were told was usually reserved for brides.

"But you're something special," Lily said with a wink.

I was happy I could give her words from her gran. I knew how much those simple words of support, knowing your loved one was still watching, meant to people.

We both selected the perfect, luscious dresses. I felt like royalty in mine as I modeled it for Audrey.

"Stan will be picking his jaw up off the floor when he sees you in that," I said to Audrey.

"And Clint won't be able to keep his hands off of you when you slip into this wine-colored creation." She said to me.

"Thanks for helping me with Irene."

"No problem, sis. I always got your back."

Chapter Sixteen

~ Joanna ~

"Boss, boss!" Micah called from the break room.

"What's up?" I ran in there to see that he had the news on, and there was a story about the Crawford family. My mouth dropped open as I realized what was happening on the screen. "They are calling it... a brawl?"

"Yeah, can you believe this?" He said, practically giggling.

We watched the footage, apparently shot from different cell phones and angles. One looked to be from Vera Beckett's and another from one of Faye's twins. Still, another was a random onlooker.

It was filmed at a shopping mall in Centerville. One of those fancy places with high-end shops that, while I could afford to shop there, I didn't. I liked my clothing as functional and straightforward; even my stage clothing was affordable.

Irene and Faye got into a shouting match which escalated into shoving, punching, and hair pulling, all with a barrage of verbal insults flying back and forth.

"Gold digger!" Faye shouted.

"You're one to talk! Whore." Irene said in return.

"I'm a whore? Who was sleeping with half the town? That wasn't me, Irene."

"Liar!"

They had attracted a large crowd, even the mall security guards were pointing and laughing. They didn't try to break it up, which actually made me a bit sad.

"And among the crowd, you can also see Vera and Dodge Beckett, children from Irene's first marriage, as well as Gavin and Flynn Meyers from Faye's fourth marriage to movie mogul, John Meyers." The news reporter said. "We also spied Oren and Viola Crawford standing off to one side, trying to blend into the crowd, but these two could never quite blend in." The reporter chuckled, and her fellow anchor joined in.

"Rachel, you are so right. The brother and sister are always just there. Not quite a part of the Crawford family, but in name only." The second anchor added.

"Wow, what a mess," Micah said as we watched the footage replay before the news changed to a different story.

"I have now met most of them. Not Vera and Dodge, but all of the others. I'm not completely surprised by their behavior." I watched it replay again. "And these are the people set to inherit millions. I really need to convince Hank to claim it, don't you think?"

"I honestly don't know. From what I've seen, these types of people always find a way to get more. More money, more fame. Whatever it is, they get it."

"That's true."

Tessa ran in. "Did you see the massive Crawford fight?"

"Yeah, we just watched it."

"It's streaming everywhere." She said.

Micah pulled out his phone. "There are already memes about it. Josh just sent me three."

"Wow, people are quick." Granted, this was footage they said from a few hours ago, but still.

"Here is a parody skit," Tessa said, whipping her phone around so we could all watch it.

It was two guys dressed as if they were Irene and Faye. They start insulting each other before getting into a highly dramatic tussle. It was obviously exaggerated for laughs.

But a part of me also felt terrible for the women. Maybe they weren't great people, but they were still people. People that had grief and children. Maybe they enjoyed the attention, and maybe they didn't.

I may never know how they felt, but myself, I would hate it. I tried to stay out of the limelight as much as possible. My stage persona was sparkly and bright, but my off-stage persona was introverted and quiet.

I had a teacher once say I went about my life quietly. That was just my way.

After our small break was over, I went back to my office to read and answer emails. We had one client cancel, so I had time in my day to relax a bit more.

I was reading a fan email. She was at the dress shop the other day, and was so thankful that I gave her closure on her sister's death. I was always glad to hear when I helped people like this. So, I typed a quick note back.

With that email sent, I sat for a moment recalling the day. Thinking of Irene's smug face melting into disbelief as I gave readings to several shoppers made me laugh even now. I wasn't always a petty person, but I did take joy in ruining her day a little.

"Ahem, excuse me." It was Hedy, but I had been so wrapped up in my thoughts and replying I hadn't heard her. I jumped, spilling my coffee in the process. "Oh, I'm so sorry, dear. I didn't mean to startle you. I seem to do that every time."

"It's okay. You'd think I would be used to spirits sneaking up on me." I laughed as I grabbed a couple of tissues to clean the spill. Thankfully it was only a tiny bit. "How are you?"

"I'm good. I haven't visited in a while, so I thought I would check in."

"Arnie's not with you?"

They only came together that one time. I was curious why. Were they not spending the afterlife together? Had they fought?

"No, no, we don't see each other much. He has gotten really preoccupied with his family and trying to convince Hank to claim the money. So, he is usually hanging around him trying to channel ghost powers or something."

"Ghost powers?" I had never heard of such a thing and was honestly curious if that was a thing.

"Yeah, you know how some ghosts are said to be able to push things off shelves or tables, or how people hear voices?"

"Yeah." Obviously, I heard voices and saw the ghosts, but I had never seen them interact with solid objects.

"He's trying to do that with Hank."

"Is it working?"

"No, he can't touch anything, and you seem to be the only living person to hear or see us."

"Have you tried to touch stuff?" I was curious as I'd never thought to ask any of the spirits if they had any special abilities. It was going on my list of things to ask.

"Yes, and no amount of concentration works. My hand just goes right through." She sighed as she tried to touch the chair in front of her. "It's frustrating because I would love to touch my son one more time."

"I'm sorry."

"I didn't know I was going to die so soon, or I would have... I don't know. I guess I should have told him about his father. Told him about his life before I changed our names. Arnie really did love him, loved us both actually, but he felt so stuck and took the path of least resistance. I didn't like it, but I, well, just accepted it. Learned to live with his decision." She sighed as she shrugged.

"I'm sorry. I know all of that was difficult and you must have felt so alone." I didn't know what else to say.

"I never loved anyone as much as I'd loved Arnold Crawford, and not because of his money. He was my soul mate, but he just couldn't let go of that money. We could have made a fine life." She smiled. "But it's okay. It's the past. Nothing I can do about it now."

"Well, then what can I do for you today?"

"I was hoping we could go talk to Hank. It would be good to tell him I love him."

"Sure. Let me try texting Al."

I sent off a message but didn't get a reply right away.

"I guess they're busy." I looked around.

"Yeah, he has always kept himself busy."

"I did talk to him recently. He had mentioned the security tapes from your house and said he had gotten a bit, but I don't know much about it."

"Oh, well, I will be interested to hear about that."

"Me too." I said. "He did say he had investigated your death, and my boyfriend, the detective, confirmed what Hank said."

"Still accidental?"

"That's the way it looks."

"I guess it was. I just don't know why I would go upstairs while cooking. That doesn't make sense. I wasn't losing my mind."

"Hank told me you were still participating in 5Ks. That's amazing."

"Oh, yes, though at my age, I didn't run them. It was kind of a slow jog." She chuckled. "But I was still agile and could slow jog circles around people half my age."

She did a few dance moves to prove her point. Of course, I couldn't speak for when she was alive, but her spirit body was quite nimble.

My text sound alerted me to a new message.

"Al says we can stop by anytime today."

"Wonderful. Do you have time?"

As she asked, Tessa stuck her head in my office. "Hey Jo, the last appointment for the day just canceled."

"That's strange. Two in one day?"

"Yeah, sadly, their mother just passed away. They were coming to see the father." She frowned.

"Ah. You'll send flowers?"

They called me a medium with a heart for a reason. I tried to have one in every aspect of my job and life. Since our job was working with dead people, sometimes the families would have more loss, and whenever we knew, we sent our condolences to them.

"Already ordered them," Tessa said and turned to leave my office.

"Oh, Tess, with no other appointments, I'm going to wrap up."

"Sounds good. I'll probably wrap up my duties and head out early too."

"Are we leaving early, boss?" Micah said, poking his head in the door above Tessa. He was well over 6 feet tall, and Tessa was a tiny 5 feet in heels. They were some of my favorite people. I smiled.

"Yep, no more appointments today. Hedy is here, so we are going to meet with Hank."

"Hi, Hedy." They both said.

"Hi, team." She smiled as I passed on her return greeting.

They didn't ask to accompany us like we had done in the past when I'd go to meet with someone at Leo's. I assume they understood this was a different type of visit, but I sure did miss those trips. I might have to start a weekly happy hour with my team.

We wrapped up, and all headed out. Percy said he would close up for us after he did a security sweep. Something he did a few times a day, with a more thorough check before and after hours.

Hedy and I arrived at Leo's. I got my usual greeting of bear hugs and a vodka cranberry. I didn't even bother to turn it down anymore, but I'd sip it politely.

Today was a bit different, though. Hank rushed over with his men to greet me. He'd never done this before.

"Joanna, I'm so happy to see you." He kissed my cheek in greeting, catching me off-guard. "Please come join me."

All eyes in the place, both Hank's men and not, were on me. I wanted to ask them what I'd done, but honestly, nobody had ever seen this side of him before. With his mother, he let his guard down. It was nice to see this other side of him.

"Is she with you?" His voice was velvet smooth, and his eyes sparkled with tears and hope.

"Yes, she is." I gestured to his right side.

They both reached towards each other. Watching them, I could see they had similar mannerisms. It was the way they moved their heads and hands, and they had the same pauses in speech.

The guys that had come forward to greet me all backed away from us slowly. Eddie gave me a wink as I watched him walk away.

I'm glad they did. It gave Hank and Hedy some privacy, and I could concentrate on what she said and could pass it on correctly.

"Mother, I miss you dearly."

"I miss you, too. They say life is short, but you don't realize just how much that's true until it's over."

"Or the person you love the most in the world is gone." He said.

I was not going to cry. I was going to remain professional. Despite fighting it, a lone tear slid down my face. I wiped it quickly before anyone saw it.

"Have you heard anything about the security footage?" Hedy asked. Getting right down to business, I thought, as I passed her message on.

"I haven't." Hank said, then frowned. "That's mom asking or you, Joanna?"

"Her."

"How did you hear about that? Did I already tell you?"

"I told her but just that you were looking at it." I said, and then for Hedy added, "Plus, she says she's been following you around."

"We still only have one day of footage that shows anything." He rubbed his chin. "A man looking in your windows. The other few days we got don't show anything unusual."

"Can I see it? Maybe I can tell who he is."

"I thought you were following me."

"Well, I'm not around you all the time. I have other people I visit." I snickered as I spoke the words. They both eyed me for a moment. I sobered and continued, keeping my emotions out of it.

"Who?"

"My bridge club friends, my personal trainer, and my jogging buddies. You know I did have a life outside of you." I smiled. She had a lot of spunk. I wish I had known her in life.

He laughed. "Of course, mother. I know how busy you were. Let's go see if Hacker can pull it up for us."

We followed Hank to a hallway and then into a dark room. The main light source was the dozen or so computer monitors. I couldn't see much else in the room; it was too dark.

"Oh, hey, boss," Hacker said as he tried to stash a potato chip bag into his desk drawer. "Jo." He nodded to me.

"Hey," I said.

"Can you pull up that footage from my mother's house? She is here with Joanna and would like to see if she can identify him."

"Oh, sure, sure." He wiped his salty fingers on his shirt. He started clicking and tapping away.

Since I'd never been back here, I looked around at the other monitors trying to figure out where each was pointed. I wasn't clear where all the buildings Hank owned were, so this gave me a glimpse.

When I saw Percy checking doors, I knew which monitor was on my office building. I smiled seeing the friendly face of my security guard.

"Alrighty, this screen here," Hacker said, pointing to the one closest to him. "This is what we have. It was three days prior."

A grainy image of a window was displayed. It wasn't great quality, but it was pretty good considering he was trying to recover it from a smoke-damaged system.

As we watched, a man wearing all black, a hoodie pulled up over his head, checked the window, and then appeared to check the one next to it, but it was partially cut off from view.

"That's it. That's all I've gotten so far that shows anything."

"I don't recognize him at all," Hedy said.

"I'm still trying, and I have gotten other days pulled, but it's mostly nothing. A bird, a shadow from a tree, daytime and then night." Hacker said.

"Thanks. Keep trying." Hank said, putting his hand on Hacker's back.

Movement on the monitor that showed my office caught my attention. My blood ran cold as I realized what was happening. I let out an animalistic scream.

Multiple assailants were attacking Percy, though he was putting up a good fight but was no match for four men.

Hank immediately got on the phone, and Al ran out of the room. I heard yells in the main room, then doors followed by the screech of tires.

I stood there helplessly as that sweet man was beaten at my office and then left on the ground. We would have been there had our last appointments not been canceled. Was it fate or something else?

Chapter Seventeen

~ Clint ~

"Hartley, Walden." Our Chief yelled across the bullpen.

"Yes, sir."

"Active scene at Hammersley Business Park on Hatfield. It's your Medium's office." He said, pointing to me.

"Shit." I grabbed my phone, and Terry grabbed his keys. "Do we know who? Is she...?"

"No, her security guard. Hank called it in. His guys just got there, and an ambulance. I know this isn't a homicide, but I want you on this since it's your girlfriend. Just collect evidence and interview witnesses." Chief called out as we ran out.

"Will do." Terry yelled back.

We hustled to his car and then down the road. I shot off a text to Jo.

"You, okay?" Terry asked me.

"Yeah, but I hope she wasn't there."

"Yeah."

My text sounded.

"It's Jo. She says she wasn't there, but she was with Hank and watched it on the security cameras in Hacker's office." I ran my hands over my face. "Damn."

She was such a soft-hearted person and I know she would have a lot of guilt, blaming herself for this attack. I'd do the best I could to reassure her.

It felt like forever before we arrived at the scene. The ambulance was pulling away, and I saw Hank, Al, Eddie, and a few of Hank's other guys milling about. Al had a sobbing Jo in his arms. I rushed out of the car and straight to her.

When Al and I locked eyes, he simply nodded to me, turned her to me, giving her back a light pat, then nodded once more before turning to speak with Terry. He was a man of few words, but he cared for Joanna and for that I was thankful.

"Oh, Clint, this is all my fault!" She collapsed into me.

I knew she would be beating herself up. I whispered to her, trying to reassure her.

I could only vaguely hear what Hank and his guys were saying to Terry.

"Four men in all black... Careful to keep their faces turned from the cameras... Catfish was unconscious but breathing." I know I missed bits, but that got me a picture of what happened, at least.

I knew Catfish or Percy for years. He had been one of Hank's "enforcers" and then started working security as he aged. He was good at getting the truth out of people and could fight with the best of them, but against four younger men, that might be a tough hill to climb for someone in their 70s.

I'd always liked him. He had a rough upbringing, had some adventures, and worked for Hank. He was an interesting guy if you could get him talking, especially over a beer or two.

Hank's activity was just this side of legal, so we mostly looked the other way. As long as we weren't finding body parts or whole bodies, we assumed he was staying within the law as he promised.

If you asked me, I assumed he'd simply gotten good at not getting caught, but I hadn't been able to prove anything. Plus, he had been good to Joanna, so I was thankful for that.

"Clint, thank you for coming." Jo finally said as she hiccuped from crying.

"Of course." I rubbed her back and squeezed her a little tighter.

Micah and his partner, Josh, arrived and rushed immediately to Jo. I let them have her, and the three of them cried, hugged, and talked together. I watched them a moment before touching base with Terry.

"Hank has the footage and is having Hacker make a copy for us now. It appears four guys might have been casing the place for a few days. Hacker is including that footage in the file."

"Good. Any ideas?"

"None. From what Hank and Al said, the guys were careful to keep their faces covered. They wore oversized hoodies that hung partially in front of their faces, and they also kept their backs turned."

"Strange. So, they knew what they were doing."

We walked around to the back door, where the attack started. Catfish had been able to escape and make it around the front before being taken down. I noted where the cameras were.

"Hacker is sending from all the cameras, including the internal even though the attack was out here."

"Okay." I nodded. There were drops of blood going from the back towards the front. "We need to get samples to see if this is all his or if maybe one of the guys can be ID'd from this."

We got right to work along with our forensic team gathering evidence and pictures. We also interviewed nearby witnesses from surrounding businesses and asked for any security footage they had.

As usual, Terry took over speaking to the media for us. He was always better on camera than I was, plus with Joanna still around, I wanted to ensure she was okay and shielded from the cameras.

After a while, Micah and Josh said they would take her home. She had to get Oakley from Janie.

"I'll call you later," I kissed her forehead softly.

"Thanks." She mumbled against my chest.

Josh wrapped his arms around her, guiding her to their car. She sat in the back seat, looking down then up just as they pulled out. I waved.

The media wrapped up shortly after, and the crowd that had gathered dispersed. Hank had one of his guys do one last security check before they all headed out.

Once we were finished with the forensic team, they headed back to the station with all the evidence. Then it was just Terry and I left at the scene. We stood talking over the top of his car.

"What are your initial thoughts?" I asked him as I looked once more at the building.

"Appears random, but who knows? We won't know until we get information on possible prints and those blood samples."

"And if Percy wakes to give his statement."

"True." He said.

A movement to our left caught my eye. I watched what appeared to be a dark figure back up into some bushes in the parking lot and then disappeared from sight. It was gone before I could react.

"Did you see that?"

Terry followed my eyes. "See what?"

I squinted but didn't see anything. There was no engine sound or headlights indicating that someone had jumped in a car. Perhaps it was just a stray dog or simply a shadow as dusk crept over the parking lot.

"I guess it was nothing."

Maybe I was tired. We had been out here for hours, and I was worried about Jo. We didn't have plans to see each other tonight, but I was going to change that.

We'd have to file our initial reports before I could leave. Forensic would take some time to return results, but I wanted to get all my witness statements down. We would go to the hospital tomorrow to check on Percy's condition and get the doctor's assessment.

For now, we were back at the station, and I was going to get this report typed up as quickly as possible. But what do they say about the best laid plans?

"Hartley." One of the patrol officers said.

"Yeah?"

"This was just dropped off for you. Guy named Hacker."

He handed me an envelope, and I could feel the USB drive in it.

"Is he still here?"

"Nah, took off but said you knew how to get in touch with him if you had questions."

"Thanks, Williams." I pulled the drive out of the envelope. I flipped it around in my fingers. I really wanted to see it, but I wanted to get out of here to check on Joanna. I sighed. "Hey, Walden?"

"Yeah?" He stuck his head in.

"Hacker dropped this off." I held up the drive.

"Let's go see what it shows."

We headed down the hall to a conference room. I plugged it into the room's computer and clicked around until the security footage played on the screen.

It pulled up the internal footage first. It looked like just a normal, quiet day. No clients.

That seemed a bit odd though. At this time of day, she would normally have clients. I made a mental note of that.

"Tessa at the desk. Micah in the break room and then going to his office..." Terry said.

"Joanna talking to herself," I said.

"Or a ghost." Terry corrected.

"I guess," I mumbled.

We watched as her assistants came to speak with her, and then they all started packing up and leaving. There was a long break in the action, but then the next movement was Percy walking through, checking all the windows and doors.

"Time difference of... about an hour from when Jo and her team left," Terry noted.

"Looks that way."

The footage then switched to outside views.

"Oh, he has it starting earlier outside," I said.

"I have the time stamp written down so we can compare," Terry said.

There were two frames playing. One of the back doors and one showing the front of the building. We didn't see much until about thirty minutes before Joanna and the team left. There was a dark sedan that pulled through the lot. It stopped near the front door, but nothing happened. It sat for a minute and then rolled out of frame.

Other than a few random leaves blowing past and a person leaving the business across from them, there was no further change until Joanna, Micah, and Tessa left later.

"Okay, that time matches the other," Terry noted.

We played it on fast forward until Percy walked out the back door roughly an hour later. He locked the door, set the alarm, and was immediately attacked by four men.

"They really are being careful to keep their faces covered and backs to the camera. Wow." I said.

"They knew where the cameras were and what to do." Terry added.

Catfish put up quite a fight, but the men overtook him with speed and small bats.

"Damn. Poor guy." Terry said when we finished watching.

"Yeah, I know Joanna feels guilty, but she really shouldn't. This may not have anything to do with her."

Unfortunately, there wasn't audio, so we had no idea if they were saying anything to him. I was just hoping it had to do with Hank and not Joanna.

"True. This could be related to Hank's business and not hers." He said. "You going to go see her?"

"Yes, I have to make sure she's okay. She's been through so much this past year."

He nodded, and we wrapped up. I secured the USB drive as evidence and then called her as I walked to my truck.

"Hey, Clint." Her shaky voice said.

"Hi, you okay?"

"I'm... okay." I could tell she wasn't, but she was trying not to show it.

"Want me to stop by?"

"I'd love that. I have dinner nearly ready if you're hungry."

"Starving."

Twenty minutes later, I was sitting at her kitchen table, passing Cheerios to both Oakley and Chewy.

"Stop feeding him," Jo said, playfully swatting my shoulder.

"He likes it," I said, scratching his ears. "This dinner is good, Jo. Thank you."

She'd made grilled chicken with roasted vegetables. Simple, but it was better than what I would have eaten on my own.

Don't get me wrong, I could cook, but cooking for one wasn't as much fun as cooking for two. My bachelor meal of choice was to make a large pot of chili and eat that all week.

"You're welcome and thank you. I had made way too much." She refilled my water and then set it in front of me. "I guess it was nerves after things with Percy. I always have to keep busy when I'm upset and nervous."

"Well, I don't think it has to do with you. This could easily be Hank's business. You know he was an enforcer for Hank before working security, right?"

"Yeah, I knew that, but it is so hard to believe when he is just this sweet old man that works in my office, or at least that's how I see him."

"I understand."

"Want to go for a w.a.l.k?" She spelled it out, but I still saw Chewy's ear perk in her direction.

"Okay."

Chewy jumped up, barking and spinning. It was his signature move.

I clipped on his leash while Jo got Oakley changed and into her stroller. Then we headed out for an after-dinner walk, something she liked to do.

There was a different vibe in this neighborhood than her last. This one was full of young families and active people. Her last was primarily retirees and empty nesters who generally kept to themselves.

Here we passed many people that greeted us. Some stopped us to talk with Joanna, Oakley, or ask about Chewy. There was a sense of community and friendliness that I loved. This was a place I wanted to live someday and raise a family.

I smiled, looking over at Joanna, pushing a giggling Oakley in her stroller. Then I looked down at the mutt with the big grin. This felt so good and right, especially after the day I'd had.

I really did hope whatever this situation with Percy was didn't have anything to do with Hank. I needed this woman to be safe. I couldn't lose another person before we ever got the chance to have a life together.

I wanted to lecture her again about staying out of trouble, but the truth was, tonight was not the night for that. She had enough on her mind without me adding to it with my own insecurities and fears.

I sighed and enjoyed the rest of our evening together. Worry could wait until tomorrow.

Chapter Eighteen

~ Joanna ~

It was several days before I got word that Percy was awake. His condition had been touch and go for a few days, but they said he was improving. The scans of his brain had initially shown swelling, so they had to relieve the pressure. Once that was done, he seemed more comfortable and woke the next day.

Clint was probably right that this was something to do with Hank's business dealings and not mine, but I couldn't shake this gut feeling it wasn't. Still, without a message from the attackers, we wouldn't know.

While Percy recovered, Eddie was here filling in for security. I was glad they hadn't sent the kid again. If someone attacked, he would be no match. But, on the other hand, Eddie was a large guy, fit and young. He might not be able to stand up to four guys with bats, but he would surely put up a bigger fight than the kid or Percy.

"Good morning, Jo," Eddie said when I arrived. He came around to give me a hug.

"Morning, Eddie. Any word about the attackers?"

"Not yet, but it's good to hear that Percy is recovering." He smiled. "And I know you, don't beat yourself up over this, okay?"

"Okay." I said, then turned to Tessa. "Hey. Schedule?"

"On your chair." She said. "You good?"

"Yeah, you?"

"Yeah."

We were both lying, but neither called the other out on the lie. It was just how our friendship worked.

I headed back to my office and was stopped by Micah. He wrapped his arms around me, and we just stood there for a moment. Then he kissed the top of my head before letting me go. I smiled weakly as we parted ways, each to our own office.

I set my purse and phone down, then grabbed my schedule out of my chair.

"Only four today." Weird, our days were usually six to seven.

I set it down and then headed to the break room for coffee.

What was happening the last few days? Cancellations and our days not booked up. I shrugged. I'm sure it was nothing. It was just a busy time of year. We'd just had Thanksgiving, so people were busy traveling, family, and shopping for Christmas or maybe Hanukkah or other holidays they may celebrate this time of year.

I tried to push thoughts of doubt on my theory down. But I couldn't help it. The holidays triggered feelings in so many with grief, and they wanted to have that connection to their loved ones, so what was happening this year?

"I'm not going to think about it," I said to the coffee pot as I poured a cup and then headed to my office to settle in for my day.

Hours later, my shorter day was over, which meant I could visit Percy in the hospital. Al had messaged me to let me know that he could see visitors now and was asking to see me.

Having been in the hospital not too long ago myself, I decided to put together a small care package for him.

So, on the way to the hospital, I pulled into a convenience store to pick up a few magazines and a treat or two. I stared at the rack of magazines for far too long.

"What does he like?" I mumbled to myself.

A guy next to me in a dark hoodie inched closer, causing the hair on the back of my neck to stand up. So, I quickly grabbed a few with cars and motorcycles on them, then before walking away, a cooking one. I internally shrugged as I kept an eye on the guy. Then before I darted away, I picked up a word search and a Sudoku one as well.

I turned up the next aisle where the candy was located so I could get a couple of his favorite candy bars. Before I could leave this aisle, another guy in a hoodie walked towards me. I turned wide-eyed towards the cashier who came around the counter towards us.

This caused the guy to back up and away. He nodded to the other guy, and they took off.

"Thank you." I said.

"No problem. I could tell they were up to no good." He nodded and returned to the register.

Picking out his candy bars, I then made my way towards the counter to pay, when I noticed a display of cards, so I selected a get-well one.

Yes, so maybe it was a little bit of guilt, but it seemed like the right thing to do.

"Be safe," the man said after I had paid.

"Thanks."

I made my way to my car, thankful it was parked close. Before driving off, I looked around, but didn't see the two men or a suspicious car.

Perhaps I should have called Clint or Eddie or Al, but since I didn't see anything strange, I didn't. Putting my car in gear, I made my way the few miles from the store to the hospital. Checking my rearview the entire way, though it didn't look as if I had been followed.

When I pulled into the parking lot, I hesitated a moment, and not because of the two random guys from the store. The problem with hospitals is that there are always a lot of dead people wandering around, and if they know who I am, I'm bombarded with requests. I hated to say no, but to date, I'd only passed on a few messages that seemed most urgent.

I grabbed the bag of goodies and headed in. I signed in at the visitor desk on his floor and then made my way through the crowded hallways. Honestly, they were probably not as crowded as they looked to me because, as predicted, there were numerous spirits hanging out.

"401, 403..." I mumbled as I walked to 415.

"Knock, knock," I said at his opened door.

The room was dark. Most of the light was coming from the window. So, I could only make out a silhouette of the objects in his room, including him lying in bed.

"Ms. Joanna, come in, come in." I heard his deep, smooth voice call to me.

"I come bearing gifts," I said but then gasped when his face came into full view. "Oh, Percy, I'm so sorry."

"No, no, it's okay. I know how it looks, but I'm lucky to be alive, from what I hear." He chuckled but then winced, grabbing his ribs.

"Are you okay?" I set the bag down on the side table and lightly touched his arm.

"Yeah, I'll be fine. I'm just sore."

"What have the doctors said about your recovery and going home?"

"They said a few days, and with the cracked ribs, I have a long road. I'll be sore for a while."

"Did the men say anything to you?" I had to know if I was responsible for his injuries, even though the rational side of my brain knew I wasn't, no matter the reason those men were there.

"They kept asking about Senator Crawford. If you had let any information slip about who the heir was."

"Oh, Percy, I'm so sorry. I knew this was all my fault." My throat tightened and I barely choked the words out.

"No, this is the business I'm in." He insisted. "I work for Hank, and I've had my share of bumps and bruises. This will heal, so don't let guilt beat you up."

"But this is because of me. How can I not feel bad for that?" Tears formed in my eyes.

"Are you the heir?" He asked firmly. "He knows and will come forward in his time, with or without the promise of money."

"You're such a kind man. I don't understand how you got into this business."

"Well, once upon a time, I wasn't so nice, and life kicked me down repeatedly, much like those thugs did. I did what I had to do to provide for myself and my family."

I simply nodded my head, but I had so many questions spinning around in it. They would have to wait. I had more important questions than being nosy about his past and family.

"Did you already speak to the police?"

"Yes, I told them they were looking for money." He chuckled, which brought another reminder from his ribs. "I keep doing that."

"Sorry, just a few more questions, and then I'll let you rest."

"No rush. I like your company."

"Aw, you're sweet." I blushed. "Why did you tell them that? It's not the truth."

"Hank's orders are clear. We don't know enough, so don't tell the police."

"Ah, so you told Hank?"

"Of course. He's my boss and signs my checks." He winked.

A nurse came in. "Hey, Mr. Percy, time for pain meds. Oh, I didn't know you had a visitor. Hi... Hey, you're that medium!"

"Yes, hi."

"Oh, I have always wanted to meet you." She gushed. "I'm Margie."

"Margie, right?" I said.

"Oh yes, that's me. My badge. That's how you know." She laughed.

"No, actually, your sister told me." I nodded to her left.

She gasped and looked. "Doris? Are you here?"

"I am, sis. Right here by you." I said.

"I never thought I would get to speak to you again. I'm so sorry for our fights those last months. I should have just supported you."

"I'm sorry too. It was all so silly. I was just scared, so I tried to push you away."

"Me too," Margie said through soft sobs.

"I have been by your side since. I was there when you held baby Aiden for the first time, when you had the lump in your breast recently, and I'll stay with you as long as possible," Doris said.

"Oh, that means so much. I know you aren't here for me, but still thank you." Margie said, wiping a tear, and then smiled. "Alrighty, Mr. Percy, I have to give you this."

She added something to his IV drip then checked his vitals.

"You should be feeling better very soon." She said to him and then turned to me. "Can I hug you?"

"Of course."

We hugged, and she thanked me again before leaving the room, telling Percy to push the call button if he needed anything. Doris followed her sister out.

"Well, I'm going to let you rest. I'm glad you're doing better."

"Thank you, Ms. Joanna. And for the gifts, I will enjoy those candies later." He winked and then closed his eyes.

I looked at him for just a second longer, then walked out and slowly walked down the hall. I pushed the elevator button and took it to the ground floor. The guilt was heavy in my heart, and I was sulking; even the holiday music playing on the ride down couldn't cheer me up.

I spied the coffee shop and decided to grab a cup of hot tea for the ride home. A little pick-me-up treat to ease the heavy burden I felt.

"Well, look at this, sis." I heard someone snarl behind me in line. Great, what now?

"Oh, it's that medium." A female voice said.

I slowly turned to find Oren and Viola in matching outfits. They truly were as weird as I'd heard.

"Hello." I greeted and then turned back to wait my turn in line.

"What are you doing here?" Oren asked.

"Probably giving fake readings, like the one she gave us." Viola snapped.

"Fake? What are you talking about? I told you what Tootie actually said." Okay, it was Hedy, but the reading itself was really from a spirit.

"Well, we went to see Madame Vanya, and she said you're a fake."

Who is Madame Vanya? Am I supposed to know her? I didn't ask. I just pulled in some confidence, which was a bit fake because I wasn't feeling too sure of myself.

"Well, she's wrong," I said firmly and then turned back to face forward again. There were only a few people between me and my tea, which would mean escape from these two.

"No, and she told us who the heir is, and we will find him and talk to him." Viola purred out.

I rolled my eyes. There is no way this Madame Vanya had told them the truth.

"Wait, why are you two here?" I asked without thinking.

"That's our business. Not yours." Oren snapped.

Oh, crap, my mind was spinning. What if they really did know? What if they knew it was Hank and were here to go after Percy again? Could they get to him? No, I had to be signed in, and I was on an approved visitor list. I'm sure he would be fine.

I tried to remain calm, offering them a fake smile, and then tried to ignore them. Finally, it was my turn at the counter. I ordered my tea, paid, and waited to the side. I watched as Oren and Viola gave the barista a difficult order and then berated him when he stumbled with their requests.

"How incompetent are you?" Oren snarled and dropped a $20 bill on the floor in the process.

It remained unnoticed, so when they huffed off instead of waiting, I swooped in and dropped it in the tip jar. To be fair, I'd seen the move in a movie or tv show, I couldn't remember which, but it was perfect for this situation.

"Thank you," the patient barista said. "They're awful."

He said that strangely as if he was familiar with them.

"Are they here often?"

"Yeah, they have a relative on the 8th floor or something. I have overheard them talking about them. Some long-term care."

"Ah, well, I hope you have a good day. Don't let them get to you. They're just bullies."

"Thanks."

I gathered my tea and left. But I kept thinking about the strange sibling pair. Who was their relative? Was any of this related to Hank and the rest of the Crawfords at all?

I'd have to research that as I wasn't even sure I knew who their parents were. I knew they were cousins to Senator Arnold, but nothing much was said about who the parents were. Maybe I could ask Hedy what she might know.

Chapter Nineteen

~ Joanna ~

Two days after my visit, Percy was released from the hospital. Hank told me Percy's oldest daughter took him to her house to recover. I didn't ask more as I knew they liked to keep family private. But, if Percy wanted me to know, he would share.

I was just happy to hear he was on the mend and out of the hospital. Not only because it meant he wouldn't be in pain, or at least soon would be. Also, there was less chance that he would see Oren and Viola or that Hank would run into them.

I thought about what they had said about this Madame Vanya. Since I'd never heard of her, I had no way to know if she was real or not. But if the two siblings had figured out the heir, that could be a problem, so the less interaction, the better.

My business was taking quite a hit, and today I had only four appointments again.

"What is going on?" I would have to research this Madame Vanya and see who she is.

But instead, I typed in Oren and Viola Crawford to see if I could find mention of parents. Articles and images of the pair came up, but nothing about parents.

Weird Siblings Make Splash at Gallery Opening, read one headline. They were dressed in matching outfits with an under the sea motif. Strange, but at least it was on theme for that specific gallery. They were featuring sea life art to raise money for ocean conservation.

Another article talked about their charity work with several places, from the hospital's memory care unit to a few animal rescues and even Harper's Angels.

"Guess that means they'll be at the gala." I sighed.

Not only did I have to face Irene and Faye there, but now this pair.

I searched through articles and images, read blogs, and social media posts, but could find nothing about who their parents were. The only thing that was clear is they were always together and often in matching outfits.

I clicked next, next, next, and it wasn't until about page seven that I finally found something. It was an old article about an accident at the Crawford home with a woman being thrown from a horse. The accident had left her nearly brain dead, but the family couldn't bring themselves to disconnect life support.

She was Arnold's cousin and Oren and Viola's mother, so technically, they were second cousins to Arnie, and their mother was his first cousin.

I skimmed through to find the date of the accident.

"Ten years ago?" That must be costing a fortune, which would be why they would want control of the inheritance.

I continued reading.

"Oh, here we go."

After a few months, she gained some function but remained in a long-term care facility run by the Creekview Hospital. Some of my past clients had mentioned that the hospital had a long-term care unit but didn't know much about it.

I sat back. This was an interesting development. I can understand why they would be at the hospital a lot now. It couldn't be easy watching your parent be a shell of the person they once were.

While my own mother drove me crazy, I did love her. She made some of my favorite meals and bought the most thoughtful gifts. She'd sometimes drop off treats for me. And now, having Oakley, she was the best grandmother.

She actually doted on all three of her grandchildren, but I got to watch firsthand how much she loved my daughter.

I sent her a text just to say I loved her. She may or may not reply, but at least it was out there.

"Hey, boss. Got a minute?" Micah knocked at my open office door.

"Yeah, come in."

He plopped down in one of my guest chairs with a sigh. "Have you heard of this Madame Vanya? Some medium working out of Buckston."

"Weird you say that. The Odd Crawfords told me about her." I said.

"Oren and Viola? When?"

"The other day when I went to see Percy. They were at the hospital."

"That's strange." He said as he sat back, stretching his long legs out in front of himself.

"Yeah, well, I just found out their mother had an accident several years ago and is in their long-term care unit."

"Ah, that makes a lot more sense, but still, wow." He said.

"Yeah, I keep running into Crawfords everywhere. Had I always and just not noticed them before?"

"It always feels like that, doesn't it? So, what did they say about this new medium?" Micah asked.

"They said she called me a fake and told them who the heir was, but they wouldn't tell me the name she gave them. Honestly, I was trying to ignore them, assuming they were just trying to upset me."

"Well, she's real, or at least she's advertising as such." He passed me a printout of an ad.

"This must be why we have been having cancellations and fewer bookings."

"Yeah, maybe." He said. "She has a commercial on radio and television."

"What?"

I could do that, but I hadn't needed to. I had advertised at first, but it had been minimal. People talked, and that was the best marketing I could have.

"I asked in the paranormal groups; nobody has heard of her before. It's like she just appeared out of thin air."

"Weird." I shrugged. "Well, I'm not going to worry too much about her right now. It's the holiday season, and there is enough business for two, and with her over in Buckston, it should be fine."

But honestly, I was worried. In just a few days, my business had been noticeably different, and if she was telling everyone that I was a fake and lying to them, that could hurt my business.

"Well, I was just curious if you'd heard of her." He stood.

"Thanks."

Micah got back to work, and I closed my browser to prepare for our one and only afternoon appointment.

It wasn't until after my appointment that I was able to search for her. Immediately, a couple of ads and a handful of articles showed up. They weren't old, just a few months from the dates on articles, but it was still a bit unsettling that I'd missed her.

"How had I missed her?"

I suppose I've just been busy with my life and living it with my rose-colored glasses. Until now, I didn't have any local competition, at least nothing that I'd heard of or that had made a difference to my business.

I had to wonder, with her suddenly popping up amid the Crawford investigation, was it related? Or was this simply a distraction? Maybe a person to give me the appearance of being a phony.

Then I saw that Vera Beckett had a video live stream all about her. Vera was basically helping promote this person.

"Ugh, of course a Crawford was involved with this woman." Well, Vera was Arnie's stepdaughter, so not technically a Crawford but close.

Ignoring Vera, I flipped through other stories about Madame Vanya. Mostly it was from one local blogger that had interviewed her a few times.

"Marketing scheme." I sighed.

It was a good idea. One I'd done in the beginning too. Once I started making some money, I hired her as one of my assistants. Best decision.

As I was thinking about her, Tessa stuck her head in.

"I'm heading out. Need anything before I go?"

"Actually, yes. Have you heard of this Madame Vanya?"

"Yeah, just recently, though, but I don't know much about her."

"Do you think we should be worried about her?"

"Nah. She is over in Buckston. It's the holiday season, so people are on vacation, traveling around." She smiled. "We will be busy again in January."

"You're probably right." I stared at the screen for a second. "Is Eddie still out there?"

"Yeah, I'll let him know you're still here."

"Thanks. See you tomorrow."

Tessa was probably right that this person wasn't anyone to worry about, but I couldn't shake an unease about her.

After Tessa left, I closed the browsers and opened my emails. I wanted to answer fan emails before I headed home.

"Might as well take advantage of the downtime." I mumbled.

"Talking to yourself." Eddie said at my doorway.

"Yep, sometimes I need an expert opinion." I smiled.

"Touché, Ms. Joanna." He chuckled. "May I come in?"

"Definitely. Come on in."

He took a seat in one of my guest chairs. "Things sure are quiet around here lately. This doesn't seem normal."

I sighed. "It's not."

"Do you know what's going on?"

"I'm trying to tell myself it's just the Christmas holidays, but I have been hearing about a new medium over in Buckston. Have you heard of anyone named Madame Vanya?"

"Can't say that I have, but I can check her out if you want me to." He sat forward.

I thought for a moment. Eddie, like all of Hank's men, was resourceful, and if anyone could get to the bottom of this, it was him.

"Um, no, actually. As tempting as it is, I will wait and see if things pick up after the holidays, but if I change my mind, you'll be the first to know."

"No problem. Anything to help." He started to stand. "How late are you working today?"

"Not too much longer. What's up?"

"Wanted to see if you wanted to join me for a cup of coffee."

"I could take a break." I grabbed my mug and stood.

"Oh, I meant like... go somewhere for coffee." He blushed. "Never mind. Just let me know when you're ready to go and I'll walk you out."

He left before I could figuratively pick my jaw up off the floor.

"What just happened?" I whispered. Had Eddie just asked me out?

The walk to my car later was going to be awkward. I might have been mildly attracted to him for a moment. I mean, he is a cross between Thor and Ironman, or other hot, sexy superhero, and with a heart of gold to boot.

I stalled in my office for as long as I could, but I had to go get Oakley. Slowly I packed up my personal things and headed out to let Eddie know I was ready to go.

He was scrolling on his cell phone when I went out. He closed it, shoving it into his pocket.

"You ready to go?"

"Yes, but you don't have to walk me out. My car is right there."

"Sorry, Jo, Hank's orders." He nodded towards one of the cameras.

"Ah. Okay." I smiled, turning awkwardly towards the door. "Eddie, I'm sorry if I've given you the wrong impression or something."

"No, no... I'm sorry. I know you are... dating the detective. I was out of line."

"No. I mean yes, I'm dating him, but no, please don't feel bad or apologize."

"I missed my chance back when we broke into our file room that one night, I guess." He laughed.

"Oh, that was a fun night." I chuckled.

It was while we were investigating Ted's death. Eddie was the head of security, so it was his idea to look through the personnel files. We had found a bit of information on Ted, but not enough for us to solve it.

"Until Hacker let me know Hank and Al were on their way to the office. We would have been so busted."

We reached my car. I pushed the unlock button and he immediately opened the door for me.

"Well, I hope you have a wonderful night, Jo." He leaned forward, kissing my cheek lightly. He winked, stepping back.

I gave a nervous wave, hopped in the car and drove off before I could do something stupid. I knew he had wanted to kiss me that night in his truck.

"Ego boosted." I giggled, looking back in the rearview to see him still standing there.

Chapter Twenty

~ Joanna ~

"New Year's Eve!" Audrey yelled, coming into my house. "Are you ready?"

She was all gussied up in a navy-blue mini dress with a boat neck and long, bishop sleeves. It had a belt in the same color tied at her waist. The hem fell just above her knee, showing her amazingly long legs. She paired it with taupe heels.

"I am!"

I was in a wine-colored floral printed dress about the same length as my sister's, but with straight sleeves that flared at the wrist. I wore it with black knee-high boots.

She and I were meeting a few friends at a club downtown. We hadn't had a girl's night in a long time. Stan had his boys, and Ms. Ruby, Tessa's mom, was here for Oakley.

"Y'all ladies have fun." Ms. Ruby called out from the living room where she had my daughter in her lap reading her a book.

Tessa was out with friends, but I was so thankful for her mother.

"Thanks for staying with Oakley." I waved from the door. "I'll have my phone!"

In Audrey's car, we blasted the radio as we drove to the club. Singing along with every song and laughing when we'd get the occasional lyric wrong.

We were meeting our friends from childhood: Taylor, Jasmine, and Sierra. They had grown up in our neighborhood, and we'd all been thick as thieves back then. Jasmine and Sierra were sisters like Audrey and me, while Taylor had three brothers.

As we had grown, we all stayed in touch, but with jobs and families, we didn't see them nearly enough. I was closer to Sierra and Taylor as they were my age, while Jasmine and Audrey had been best friends.

With each get-together, we'd always promise to do it again soon, but it would be months or longer between seeing each other.

We parked in the overflowing lot across from the club. The street, sidewalks, and parking lots were packed with partygoers and music blasting from every direction.

"Jasmine messaged. They're waiting for us by the coffee shop on the corner." Audrey shouted over the crowd.

I nodded, grabbing her arm so I didn't get lost as we fought through the lively crowd. People danced and greeted each other with hugs and high-fives. We received our fair share of greetings from strangers. It was a fun vibe.

"This is awesome!" I yelled to Audrey.

She mouthed something that I missed.

As we neared the coffee shop, it was obvious why they picked this spot. It was less crowded, and you could actually find people. We all did the girl squeal thing and ran to hug, greeting each other with happy new years and don't-you-look-lovely comments.

"I didn't know it would be this busy." Taylor yelled after the greetings. "I've never been out here for New Year's Eve."

"I haven't been in several years. It has grown." Sierra said. "Remember that one year, Jo?"

"Yeah, that was an exciting night."

It had only been the two of us then as both Audrey and Taylor had new babies at home, and Jasmine had been on her honeymoon. So, the two lonely single girls hit the town and nearly ended up arrested for a complete misunderstanding.

"I had no idea that corner was for hookers." Sierra laughed.

"Yeah... we were just looking for a party, not *that* kind of party."

"Undercover cops." Sierra rolled her eyes. "I'm glad they believed us."

We made our way back through the crowds and down the street to Brights. The newly opened club had a long line that we couldn't even see the end of from here. We were trekking past the door when we had a bit of luck. One of the bouncers recognized me.

"Jo!"

"Matt?" He was one of Hank's guys. "I didn't know you worked here."

"A new gig. Hank owns the club."

"He does? Wow."

He looked down the line to the end and then to us with a big smile. "Y'all can go right on in, ladies."

"Matt, you're a sweetheart." I kissed his cheek as we went by.

"Hey, that's not fair! We've been waiting." Came the shouts.

Matt silenced them with the threat of not letting them in at all. If only the folks outside knew what it took for me to get this relationship with the owner, they might not want to trade with me.

Not that I had regretted my friendship with Hank, but there were moments it was scary, and I'd feared for my life. On the other hand, there were many times he and his men had rescued me, so that part worked in my favor. Plus, this was a nice perk indeed. Maybe they should be jealous.

We stepped from the loud street into the even louder club. We held hands or hooked arms to keep together, laughing and pulling each other through the crowd.

I could feel the beat of the music thumping and bumping in my soul. The lights were bright and flashing randomly as if dancing with the music. A giggle escaped as I swayed and bopped through the club towards the bar.

We ordered a round of drinks, then scooted to the edge of the dance floor to watch and enjoy our beverage. Talking wasn't possible, so we danced along with the music, enjoying each other's company and watching the crowd.

There was a tap on my shoulder. I turned to find the kid from security.

He leaned to my ear. "Hank has asked for you and your friends to join him." He gestured towards a roped-off section.

I nodded and then gestured for everyone to follow. I almost lost the kid a few times in the sea of people, but he would stop or move the masses as he wished. Maybe I'd underestimated this kid. What was his name? Aiden or Ace or Andrew? Something with an A.

We reached the area, and I instantly noticed Al, Trent (or T as the guys called him), and a few others that I'd worked with. Thankful Eddie wasn't here. It could have been uncomfortable for us both.

Of course, there was Hank with a red-headed beauty on his arm, but he pushed her aside to greet us.

"Joanna! I'm so glad to see you here." He kissed my cheek. "What do you think of my new place?"

"It's loud and... bright!" I laughed.

"Ha, that's the point. Good for conducting business." He said with a wink.

Oh boy, what did that mean? I would never know because I wasn't going to ask.

He then greeted Audrey. He had met her a few times and remembered her.

"How are those handsome boys of yours?" He asked.

"Growing like weeds. You're sweet to remember." She touched his arm gently.

I then introduced him to our friends.

"Nice to meet you, ladies." He smiled brightly at them. "Any friend of Joanna is a friend of mine."

"Thank you!" They all said.

"Well, sit or dance. I have a private bar. Everything is on me." He gestured towards his bar. "Now, please excuse me. Gillian gets jealous."

He turned, making a big gesture to greet her, wrapping her in his arms and kissing her neck. She smiled at him, then gave me an evil death stare.

Ignoring her because I knew my relationship with Hank was mostly business. But I had every intention of enjoying this VIP treatment.

We headed to the bar for fresh drinks. Darius was behind the bar, so I didn't have to order. He just kept my favorite coming.

Hank's guys were fun dance partners and challenged us to a few rounds of pool as we partied until midnight.

"3... 2... 1! Happy New Year!"

The place went crazy with shouts as glittery, shiny confetti was shot from air cannons out over the crowd, and balloons were dropped from the ceiling.

Our group jumped and cheered.

"I'm so glad to be spending this time with you, ladies," I shouted.

"Me too," Jasmine yelled.

We hugged each other.

"Should we start heading out?"

"It's still a bit early for New Year's night, right?" Sierra asked. "Can't we hang here?"

We looked over to Hank. He was still partying it up with his gal and guys, so I shrugged.

"Yeah, let's stay for at least another round." I gestured to Darius. "I'm just going to hit the ladies' room. Anyone need to go?"

"I'll go with you." Taylor offered, but the rest declined.

We hooked arms as the crowd was still quite large, and we swam our way towards the restrooms. On the way, I accidentally bumped into a number of people, but only one gave me the creeps. He looked vaguely like the hoodie guys from the convenience store and now that I thought about it, they were dressed like the guys who attacked Percy.

I shook it off because he didn't say anything, just nodded and moved away from me. Each time spirits had come to me with a possible murder, I would get extremely paranoid. This had to be one of those crazy, paranoid moments that didn't mean anything.

Unfortunately, when we arrived at the restrooms, there was a long line. Not a complete surprise.

We chatted the best we could over the noise as we waited, and just before we would finally make it from the loud club to the inside of the restroom, a familiar face came out.

It was Vera Beckett. She was holding her phone out. Apparently, live streaming her every move including her bathroom activities.

"And here we are again, my loves, in the new club, Brights!! Woohoo." Then her eyes locked with mine. "Well, well... look who we have here. Joanna the medium with a heart."

She turned, so the phone's camera had me in the shot.

"Or should I say fake medium with a heart? Am I right? My mother went to her, so she could connect with my dead stepfather, gag, and Ms. Joanna couldn't do it. Can you believe it?" She laughed. "What do you have to say for yourself?"

"No comment." I had nothing to prove to her or her millions of fans.

"Sounds like guilt to me! What say you, folks?" She started reading off comments from people online. "You're so bad, DJSmokes88! Oh, so true, FaePeople515."

"Not that I need to justify my life or business to you, but I have proven time and again that I'm real. Ask your mother about her shopping trip to Rosie's Glamorous Gowns, or better yet, since your mom would probably lie, go ask the saleswomen that work there."

"I think we've hit a nerve, folks!" She cackled. "Relax, it's a joke. It's New Year!"

"It might seem funny to you, but that is my job. If you tell people I'm fake, I will lose business."

That set her off in a fit of laughter. "You're worried about your business more than helping people? That's rich. I hope you're all hearing this. You're a money-grubbing fake."

"I help people." That was all I could get out before the line moved, and I was inside the restroom now. I stared back at Vera as the door closed, taking her from my sight. "What in the...?"

"Don't worry about her." Taylor said. "The only people that watch her are teens and people with low self-esteem. Nothing to worry about."

I nodded, but I couldn't help feeling hurt and concerned. My business had already taken a big hit from this new medium, and now this. Vera was a viral hit. So many people would see that. Plus, the internet could spread things faster than a wildfire.

I also couldn't ignore the fact that Vera had been promoting Madame Vanya. It had to mean something.

As we were heading back to the VIP section, Taylor was leading the way with me too wrapped up in my own thoughts. I didn't notice the two guys in dark hoodies approach me until one grabbed my arm. That caused Taylor to stop when she felt the resistance.

"Watch your back, medium." The one snarled. His hood covered his face perfectly, just like the guys that attacked Percy. It was the guys from the store and earlier too. I tried to scream, but the sound caught in my throat.

As fast as they were there, they were gone.

"What was that about?" Taylor said at my ear.

"The usual... threats on my life." I shrugged, but a cold chill traveled through me. I hadn't even done anything, well, not much, this time. I couldn't help it if people told me things.

We rejoined our friends to finish our night out. We ended up at an all-night diner, but I couldn't shake the encounters with both Vera and the hooded men.

Chapter Twenty-One

~ Clint ~

I was finally heading over to meet with Hank about his mother and father's deaths.

"Wow, that still seems weird," I said to myself.

Never in a million years would I have connected the Senator and Creekview's Mob Boss. However, after Joanna said it, I could see the resemblance. I can't believe nobody else had picked it up by now. If you pulled up a picture of the Senator at 58 years old and Hank now, they could be nearly twins.

I felt we were close to solving this, but I was missing a few more pieces. This is what I loved about the work I did. A puzzle that needs to be solved. I had to use logic, skills, and it challenged my mind.

I pulled into Leo's parking lot. A place I knew all too well. The exterior was unassuming with its windowless brick and stucco façade and a weather-beaten sign reading Leo's Bar. If you didn't know it was here, you could almost drive right by.

The inside was dated, and that date was roughly 1974. It was dark and dank smelling of stale beer and mold. But with Hank here, he tried to at least keep things in good repair. The leather seats didn't have rips in them. The dark wood paneling on the walls was clean and intact, and there was always good food and drinks.

Stepping inside, I saw the place was full of mobsters waiting on their next assignment from the boss or relaxing after completing their most recent one.

"Hartley." A couple of the men shouted.

"Can I get you a beer?" Darius asked from behind the bar. "On the house."

"On the clock, so just a water?"

"One beer won't hurt ya, but one of the bar's best waters coming up." He rolled his eyes and turned to prepare my lame drink order.

I stood there waiting to be called to Hank's table. That is the way this worked. Leo's was where Hank did all his business and entertained his lady friends in between other business.

Despite their greeting when I entered, a few of his men gave me a bit of side-eye. I hadn't had too many issues with them recently, but I did a time or two when I was a patrol officer. I nodded to them, and they slowly returned the gesture before going back to their game of pool or drinks.

After a few moments of waiting, Hank's date departed the booth, then Al stepped forward to call me back towards Hank's booth. I grabbed the tall glass of water that Darius clunked down on the bar earlier and headed over.

"Have a seat, Detective," Hank said.

I slid into the booth across from him. "Thanks. Glad we're finally able to connect."

"Yes, me too. So, what do you have for me?"

"Well, I know Jo told you about the autopsy, so I made a copy of it for you." I pushed the drive over to him. He took it with a nod and handed it to Al who immediately departed into the dark hallway that led to Hacker. I knew the room well, having been back there a few times. "Now, I know you have something for me as well, right?"

"Of course. Al is getting it from Hacker now."

"I appreciate that. I think we are close, but I can't quite connect the dots. I'm working on warrants to search and secure property from the Senator's house, possibly his sister, Faye, and the cousins. I believe his wife has his computer, cell phone, and other items we need to put this together."

"What about my dear mother? Are you researching hers as thoroughly?"

"I'm hoping if I find what happened to the Senator, it will help me with hers also. Her autopsy and the arson investigation just don't leave a lot of suspicion like Crawford's does."

"Sadly, I have to admit you're right on that. I just hope in this footage, we can put it together. I do so miss her." He said, his normal stoic composure slipping a bit. "Her death has never sat with me right, and the thought of it being malicious would haunt me. I could have, should have upgraded her security equipment. I run a security company, for crying out loud." He slammed his fist down.

"I understand, and I hope that we can figure it out. Closure is important, but you can't beat yourself up about it." Damn, was I starting to think like Joanna with this closure business?

Maybe I would need to talk to her about Monica. It would be weird having an intimate conversation with my former while my current translates the messages back and forth. But perhaps it would give me a fresh perspective on my future with Jo.

Hacker came running out with some printouts in hand and a pipsqueak of a kid on his heels. I recognized him as the one that fills in sometimes with security. I knew he was around 22 years old, but he looked like he hadn't even hit puberty yet.

"Boss, I compared some of this footage. Take a look," Hacker said.

He slammed the pictures down on the booth and passed me another USB drive. The images were a bit blurry and grainy from being screen grabs from video, but it was clear what we were looking at. The same hooded bandits that attacked Percy.

Hank grabbed the pictures and quickly flipped through them. Then he looked up at Hacker.

"Where is this?"

"Senator's house. Your mother's, which you know, and of course Joanna's office." Hacker pointed to the pictures in Hank's hands. "These are from around Jo's house, and these are some randoms from around town where I just happened to see them. Well, Ace did." He nodded to the kid.

"Hooded man. Hooded man. Hooded man." He slammed them down one at a time. "This is our connection."

I didn't know he could see at Joanna's house. That surprised me, though it shouldn't. Hank was resourceful, and Hacker could get into any system he wanted, so perhaps this was one of the city cameras or a nearby neighbor's system. I wouldn't ask because what I didn't know couldn't hurt me... much.

"Now, we just need to figure out who the heck they are," I said.

Hank looked at Hacker and Ace, then with a flick of his wrist, they went off to get to work on that piece.

"Now, Detective, about Ms. Joanna, are you doing everything you can to keep her safe?"

His question caught me off guard, causing me to sit back. "Of course."

"Good, because you don't have a great track record with that."

"Well, neither do you, I might add. She has had trouble with your men right there."

"Fair enough." He stared at me with a look I couldn't read. "Then we will both work hard to keep our favorite girl safe."

"Agreed. Anything else with this case?" I asked him.

"None at the moment. Finding out who these men are will be our top priority, and you work on the Crawford family. Let me know if you have trouble with the warrants. I have a few favors I could call in." He raised a hand, signaling we were done.

Al didn't do anything exactly threatening, but his body tensed ever so slightly as if ready to make me leave if I argued. I had no plans to fight, as I had a lot of respect for Al.

He had been a great friend and protector to Joanna and Oakley. And I knew what he did to care for his mother and sisters. He was good people as far as I was concerned. Not to mention, he was nearly twice my size, and I wasn't exactly a small guy.

I nodded and stood to leave.

"Oh, and Clint, you better marry that girl soon before someone else does." He winked, then signaled to his latest, young, hot date to rejoin him. She giggled, sliding in next to him, wrapping her slender arms around him.

I walked out into the daylight and took a deep breath. That went well, but I still didn't have what I really wanted. The answer.

I fingered the drive in my pocket. I knew it would be all the security footage that I didn't already have, but they also said it would have some files.

The door to Leo's flew open, and the kid came out carrying a box.

"Oh, good, I caught you." He thrust the box forward. "Mr. Al said we forgot to give you this."

"What is it?" I looked in the box to find a laptop, an external hard drive, a notepad, and some file folders. There was a strong smell of smoke and burnt plastic. "Is this from Hedy's house?"

"It is. Hacker and I cleaned up the equipment enough to get them up and running. All her history is on those. Mr. Hank thought it would help you with anything you found at the Senator's house.

Perhaps any communications. We didn't see anything, but at the time, we weren't looking for... well, we didn't know."

"Well, alright, thanks. Ace, was it?"

"Yes, sir. It's my pleasure. Anything for Ms. Joanna." He blushed and fled back into the bar.

Ah, so he might have a little crush on my girl. I chuckled as I carried the box back to my truck, then headed back to the station to check the progress of my requests and to dig through this box.

Chapter Twenty-Two

~ Joanna ~

"Order for Joanna?" the lady at the counter of my favorite deli said.

"That's me. Thank you." I took the bag.

"Hey, you're that medium."

"Yes, I am." As I was in the habit of doing, I looked around for someone to step forward, but no one did.

"Are you a fake like they're all saying?"

"No, of course not." Though I couldn't prove it right now. Since I didn't have time, and there was no spirit stepping forward, I felt my best course of action was to grab my food and leave.

Without giving her a chance to say more, I did just that, but with one awkward smile to her as I did. Back on the street, I exhaled sharply. What is happening to me? Granted, I had once faked things, but I had done it so well that people believed me. I'd built a thriving business on it.

Who are they? What exactly are they saying? Does this have something to do with Madame Vanya again?

I shook off the encounter and got my mind in the zone to face my mother. I loved her, but she knew how to push my buttons.

Instead, I would focus on a happier moment with her, like when we celebrated Christmas a few weeks ago, probably because I hadn't had to interact with my mother too much. Plus with her three grandchildren around, Mom was in a friendly mood.

Lunch had been at my parents' house. It could be quite a large and loud affair with my sister and her family, our aunts, uncles, and cousins, plus all of the new generations.

Having a child there this year, it was fun to watch her interact with the other littles and try to keep up with the bigger ones. Harris was such a sweet, proud cousin. He had taken her by the hand to show her around and wanted to include her in everything.

"I know she can't understand all the games, Auntie Jo, but I like when she giggles." He laughed and helped her with a toy she was playing with.

"Well, I know she loves you and enjoys you teaching her." I kissed the top of his head. He squirmed but let me.

Mostly for the picture's sake, I'd bought Oakley a beautiful red and green tulle and lace dress. I paired it with white tights with Christmas trees on them and black patent leather Mary Jane shoes. She had just enough hair that I could do little pigtails. I added matching red and green ribbons that she left in long enough for me to get a few blurry pictures. The ones sans ribbons all turned out perfectly, though, so it wasn't a complete loss.

I sent them to Caitlyn in prison, including the blurry ones, as I knew she'd get a kick out of them. I hadn't been able to visit with her in a few months, and I know she loved getting updated pictures of Oakley. I sent letters weekly and always included fun stories and photos.

Now just a few weeks after that, I pulled up at my parents' house with a sack of sandwiches and without their granddaughter. I was sure to get a tongue lashing for not having her, but I'd promise a day with her soon.

My childhood home hadn't changed much over the years. The big oak in front was a lot larger, and the outside had gotten a new color of paint, but it was still home.

I noticed their Christmas lights were up. I chuckled. It had been two weeks since the new year; they should be down. I'm sure they got a letter or soon would about their homeowner's violation.

"Knock, knock," I said as I pushed the door open.

"In the kitchen." My mother yelled out.

"You know your Christmas lights are still up," I said, walking in and setting the bag on the counter.

"I know. I know. The company that put them up won't return my calls. Those fly-by-night places are so annoying." My dad muttered. He stood up and stormed out to the garage, the door slamming behind him.

"Whoa." I stared. My dad was always so even-tempered. This must really be bothering him.

"You shouldn't have brought that up. It's a sore spot with him today." My mother said as she peeked in the bags.

"Have you asked Stan for help? Or I can ask Clint to come over. I'm sure either would be happy to do it. Clint took mine down."

"I don't need help. I can do it myself." My dad growled as he stomped through, carrying the 10-foot ladder from the garage. It banged on the floor and walls as he went through.

"Charlie, you can't do that. Wait for one of the boys to come help." My mother chastised him.

"Yeah, Dad. Let me text them both and see who can come over."

"No, no, I'm doing this. We already got a letter from the HOA. So, I'm getting it done today."

We heard him go out the front door and slam it behind him.

"He can be so stubborn." My mother said with a sigh. "Text Stan and Clint to see if one of them can come to help him."

"Alright." I typed out the message. "I didn't realize it would set him off like that."

"You didn't know." She said. "Let's get this food plated. I'm sure he'll be back in a minute when he realizes it's too hard for him."

I could hear his heavy footsteps as he stomped around on the roof. With each bang and pow, I was sure he would come through the ceiling. I could count on one hand the number of times I'd seen my dad lose his temper like this. I guess this really was a thorn in his side.

My text chimed. "Oh good, Clint can come right now." I replied, then set my phone on the counter.

"Go tell your dad so he can come in and stop this silliness."

I reached the door just as I heard a loud crash, and then heard my dad yell out in pain.

"Mom! Come quick."

I ran to where my dad was lying in the yard. He was moaning, and the ladder was on top of him. I pulled it off. He had blood oozing from an ugly gash on his head, and his left leg was bent at an odd angle. Obviously broken from the fall. Those were the only visible wounds I could see, but no telling what else was wrong.

"Dad, what hurts? Can you stand?" I knew the answer but didn't know what else to say in my panic.

"Leg... no." He moaned. "There was a flash of light and... then I fell." He groaned and writhed in pain on the ground.

"Okay, be still." I stood. Flash of light, probably a car windshield or something. "Mom, I will get something to clean his head a bit. Call for an ambulance."

She stood there in shock for a moment, wringing her hands.

"Mom, help him. Make the call!" I demanded as I ran back into the house for a damp cloth.

"Oh, Charlie..." I heard her mumble before the door shut behind me.

While I was inside, she recovered long enough to call for an ambulance. I held his hand and tried to keep him calm while we waited. A few neighbors started gathering as we waited. Everyone tried to be helpful, but we really needed to wait for professionals.

I was just trying to hold it all together between keeping the crowd at bay, my mother calm, and my dad from going into shock. Thankfully the ambulance showed up at the exact moment Clint did.

"What happened?" He said, jumping out of his truck.

"He was being stubborn and thought he could take them down by himself." My mother said, tears streaming down her face.

My dad tried to correct her as he mumbled about a flash of light again, but the EMTs were taking his vital signs and getting his leg stabilized. He couldn't focus enough to explain.

Once they had him ready, they loaded him into the ambulance, Mom close to his side. She climbed in, never letting go of his hand.

"Clint and I will meet you there," I called out as I thrust my mother's purse to her, and the doors closed. Then I watched as it rolled down the street. A fresh batch of tears formed in my eyes and a lump in my throat.

"You okay?" He said, pulling me into him.

"No. I shouldn't have let him do it. I should have tried harder to stop him." I choked.

"It's not your fault." He whispered. "He's a grown man, and you did try to get him help; he just didn't wait."

Still, I couldn't help but feel guilty. I stared out the truck window, watching Creekview blur as I quietly sobbed my way to the hospital that I was becoming all too familiar with.

I did manage to pull myself together enough to message Audrey, as I knew Mother would be too busy getting things settled at the hospital. She replied that she'd meet us there as soon as she could get someone to watch her boys.

Clint allowed me space to have a little emotional breakdown. He simply reached over and squeezed my knee while we drove.

When we arrived, he parked in the visitor lot. He held my hand as we walked in. I was so thankful to have him here with me.

I looked up at him, smiling weakly through my tears.

"Let's find a restroom so you can freshen up before you face your mother." He whispered as he wiped a few tears with his thumb.

"Okay," I mumbled.

After washing my face and doing a few breathing exercises with my reflection, I made my way to the emergency room to find where my father was and how he was doing.

"Hi, I'm looking for Charles Webber. He was brought in by ambulance. Fall from a roof." I could barely get the words out.

The nurse smiled and then typed in the computer. "You're his daughter, right? They said to expect you. Ah, yes. They have him in the back. I will let them know you have arrived. Please have a seat."

We turned towards the crowded waiting area, then waded to the far corner, finding the only two open seats.

It wasn't too long ago I was in this same waiting room in almost this exact same seat, waiting on news about Al when he had been shot.

I hadn't come when they brought Percy because Hank said it was best that I wait. After seeing how ruthlessly those men had gone after him, I didn't disagree, so I let Micah and Josh drive me home.

Clint held my hand as we waited to hear news on my dad's status. Wherever my mother was waiting, she would be a basket case. I wish I could be with her now. She didn't handle emergencies well. My dad had always been the rock of the family, and now with him down, she would crumble.

"Joanna," I heard my sister's familiar voice call out. She worked her way through the crowded ER. "What happened? Have you heard anything?"

"He slipped off the roof and no, nothing. He was at least conscious when they loaded him up. A cut on his head and a broken leg at the minimum."

"What about Mom?"

"I haven't heard anything from her."

"Thanks for bringing her over, Clint," Audrey said, smiling at him.

We sat and waited for at least another hour. Since Oakley was with Janie, I made arrangements with Micah and Josh to relieve her. She had plans tonight, or she would have happily kept her. But the fun uncles were more than happy to have her for a few hours, so I could focus on my father.

Micah had a key to my house, so they would let Chewy out and make sure everyone was cared for until I could get home. They were lifesavers.

Finally, my mother, eyes puffy and face pale, being escorted by a nurse, came out with the news. The nurse handed her off to us with a brief smile and an offer to help if we needed anything. But unfortunately, I had missed what she said her name was.

"He has a broken leg that will require surgery. The gash on his head is being stitched up now. Unfortunately, his blood pressure is erratic, likely from the injury and stress, so they are trying to get that stable before they can do the surgery, which will likely be tomorrow." Mom said, her voice catching a few times. She had a wad of crumpled tissues in her hand. She smoothed one enough to wipe at her eyes. "What do I do without him tonight?"

"You'll come stay with us tonight, Mom." Audrey offered before I could. Honestly, I was relieved that my sister beat me to it.

"Okay. Do you mind if we wait until Dad is moved to a room before we leave?"

"Of course." Audrey answered. "Stan has the boys, so I'm all yours."

"Oakley is with Micah and Josh, so I'm going to stay awhile longer too." I turned to Clint. "But, you don't have to stay unless you want to."

"Actually, I'll go to their house." He turned to my mother. "And get the lights down for you, so that is one less thing you have to worry about."

"That's a good idea." I passed him my spare key to the house. "Thank you so much."

"Is there anything else I can do for you while I'm there?"

"Um, no... oh, did the food get put away?" Mom asked.

"We handled it before coming here. No worries." Clint said.

"Okay, thank you so much."

He nodded, wished us luck, and promised to be careful. Before leaving, he turned to me. "Let me know once you're home."

"I will."

Then it was just the three Webber girls waiting to hear how their family patriarch was doing.

Chapter Twenty-Three

~ Joanna ~

It had been two days since my dad's accident. His surgery to fix his leg had been successful, and they had kept him an extra night to ensure his blood pressure remained stable.

With his release today, the plan was for me to pick up Mom from my sister's house, where she'd been staying. Then we'd go pick up Dad together. I could then ensure that they were settled at home.

I pulled up in front of Audrey's house with plenty of time to get Mom and head over. I knocked on the door and was surprised when Harris answered.

"Should you be answering the door?" I asked. He was now 6 years old, but given the issues I'd had this past year, I couldn't help but think how unsafe the world was.

"It's okay. Mommy asked me to watch for you and let you in when you got here."

"Ah, okay then." I hugged him as he tried to squirm away.

"Ew, Auntie Jo, I'm too old for hugs now."

"Since when?" He let me hug him at Christmas.

"It's a new year, and it's a new me."

"Well, aren't you sassy this morning." I laughed. "Where's Grandma?"

"Still in bed and refusing to get up." He rolled his eyes. "Mommy has been trying to get her up all morning."

"Oh boy. Okay."

He followed me as I turned down the hallway to the guest room. I could hear Mom whining and moaning while Audrey was using her best mom voice, trying to motivate Mom into action. From what I could hear, it was like their roles were reversed.

"You have to go get Dad. He needs you now." Audrey said.

"I have a headache, and my stomach hurts." Mom groaned to try to make it believable.

Our mother's infamous trait was faking sickness to get attention or when she was upset. I swear she was a grown toddler. How she raised us was amazing.

"You always do this. You need to suck it up and be there for Dad like he has always been there for you."

Go, Audrey, I thought as I stood eavesdropping from the hallway. I smiled down at Harris. Should he be listening to this? Oh well.

I continued to listen, and yes, I was being a chicken hiding outside the room, but to be fair, Audrey had it handled. Plus, I hated dealing with one of Mom's tantrums. Audrey was so much better at it. She did have a few years of mommy experience more than me, plus she'd known Mom longer, what with being the older sister.

"I don't wanna." The bed squeaked; Mother had likely flipped herself around for dramatic effect.

"Too bad. You are a grown-ass woman that needs to take care of her husband."

"Don't curse at your mother." Mom snapped.

"Then act like a mother and a wife," Audrey snapped back, then opened the door to the bedroom to find me standing there. "How long have you been standing there?" Audrey barked at me.

"I just walked up." Lying to avoid the wrath of Audrey.

"She's been here longer than that," Harris said.

"Hey..." I said, turning towards him with a chuckle and then back to Audrey. "No, seriously, barely a minute. I didn't want to interrupt."

"Well, I need help. She's impossible." Audrey stomped off.

"I doubt I can do better." I stepped in to find Mother with the blankets up to her nose, her hair going in fifty different directions and looking like she slept in her makeup. "Mom, what's going on?" I used my best, most soothing tone.

"I'm scared."

"Of what?"

"Being alone in that big house with your father. What if something happens again? We can't take care of that big, ole house anymore. It's a pain to clean. I don't even go upstairs anymore. Your dad does once a month to just check the plumbing and change the filters, but that's it."

"Okay, well, maybe it's time to look at one of those retirement communities. Some of them have on-site assistance and nursing." I took her hand. "But, we can work on that later. Right now, let's go get Daddy and get him settled at home. I can come to check in regularly, and I'll look into a home-care nurse until he is back on his feet completely. Sound like a plan?"

She nodded.

I called to tell them we were a bit delayed but would be there shortly. Mom went and smoothed out her hair, applied her makeup, and got dressed in a satiny peach blouse and navy slacks. Finally, she added her ever present pearls.

Now this is the way Mom usually looked.

"Ready?" I asked.

"Yes."

Audrey walked us out but didn't say much to either of us. I put Mother's packed bag into the trunk of my car. I had packed it for her while she dressed.

"Shouldn't you tell Audrey thank you?" I prompted.

"Thank you for allowing me to stay with you. I appreciate it."

Audrey mumbled a reply that I didn't catch, but I think I heard something about ungrateful and never again. I stifled a laugh as I drove away.

We were over an hour late in picking up Dad. As we were walking in, I remembered Dad had asked me for a favor.

"Dad asked for coffee, so why don't you go meet him upstairs, and I'll duck into the coffee shop and grab us each a cup."

"Okay. Will you come up after?"

"Yes, unless you say y'all are coming down, then I'll meet you back here. Okay?"

"Okay." She started to walk away but looked back like a scared child, her hands clasped together and tears forming.

Sometimes I really worried about my mother's mental health. Perhaps once Dad felt better, I would speak to him about it. Until then, I'd keep an eye on her and ensure the home health care provider I hired could help me.

I stepped into the coffee shop. As I'd witnessed before in this hospital, there was the usual long line. I smiled at some people nearby but mostly kept to myself. There were many dead people milling about, so I didn't want to call attention to them if I could avoid it.

"Well, well, well. Look who we have here, once again, Oren." I heard the piercing sound of Viola Crawford's voice.

"Are you following us, Medium?" Oren growled.

"Not at all. My father is here. He had an accident." An over-share, perhaps, but I felt it was needed right now.

"Humph. Likely story. What was it last time?" Viola scowled as she looked me up and down, followed by an eye roll and a flip of her hair, just to top off her annoyance at my presence here.

"My security guard had been attacked. You wouldn't know anything about that, would you?" Why not? They were being jerks; I could be too.

They both gasped.

"No, why would you think we would do that?" Viola asked, hand over her heart as if genuinely offended.

"Because you seem to care an awful lot about me and my business. And if I might ask, why are you always here?" Of course, I knew the answer, but I thought I would push my luck.

"That's none of your business," Oren said.

"Our mother," Viola said at the same time. They both looked at each other.

"Why did you tell her that?" Oren said.

Viola lowered her voice and looked around. "She might as well know. It's not like it's some big, huge secret. We are Crawfords. Everything we do is plastered everywhere."

As if the universe wanted to put an exclamation point on her statement, there were sudden camera flashes all around us and shouts of their names.

"Crap. They always find us." Viola winced and tried to hide her face. "I thought we'd been so careful this time."

They both looked truly uncomfortable and embarrassed by the sudden cameras. I stepped in front of them.

"Get out of here. This is a hospital. Show some respect." I yelled to the paparazzi.

"It's Joanna, the medium with a heart!" One shouted.

Suddenly all the cameras were on me.

"Well, that backfired," I whispered, backing away from them.

My phone chimed. It was my mother saying they were on their way downstairs. I hadn't gotten the coffees. I hadn't gotten to speak more to Oren and Viola.

I looked around, trying to decide my best course of action. After looking at Viola and Oren's wide-eyed expressions, I knew they wouldn't be of much use, so I decided to run for it. They followed suit, and we tried to get behind the safety of the hospital security.

The guard stepped forward and forced the paparazzi out of the building.

"You can wait outside, but not in here." He said.

"Thank you, Joanna." Viola turned to me as we all backed up further into the hospital lobby. "Maybe we've underestimated you."

"They call me the medium with a heart for a reason." I smiled.

She pulled me back even more from the crowd. "Our mother had an accident several years ago. She requires a lot of care. She basically has the mental state of a two-year-old child. This place has the best care for her."

Tears were forming in the corner of her eyes. She obviously cared for her mother. I had only met them in person a few times, but this was a new side to them that I don't even think the media had caught. I touched her arm. She looked up with a smile.

"And that's why we were concerned about who this heir is. He could take away the money we need for our mother. I don't know why our grandparents or great-grandparents set up the family trust the way they did. Maybe once upon a time, it made sense, but it doesn't any longer, and we just want to be able to care for our mother for as long as she has left the best that we can." Oren filled in.

I guess his reservations about me had changed too. Finally, they were willing to tell me their family secrets.

"Can you understand our feelings?" Viola pleaded.

"I can. I really can. If I could help you, I would." Of course, I could, but it wasn't my secret to share.

My heart hurt for them, and I really wished I could help them, but my loyalty was to Hank. If he wanted people to know, he would step forward. Until then, I had to respect his wishes.

Viola narrowed her eyes on me. Something that seemed to be a trademark move for her, or did she have a secret power that involved mind reading?

"I think you could be lying, but I'm going to choose to believe you. Only because you stood up for us back there. Not something people do. We're the weird Crawfords, after all." I tried to hide my surprise at her words. "We hear it. We know people say it, and that's fine. We're who we are."

The elevator opened, and out came my parents. A nurse was pushing my father in a wheelchair. My mother was smiling, carrying my father's things, and chatting away. She looked much calmer and put together now that she was again by her husband's side.

"If I hear anything, I will let you know, but there are my parents, and I need to get my father home." I smiled and quickly made my way to my parents' side.

We got Dad settled in the car, and then I pulled out of the hospital parking lot.

"Where are the coffees?" Mom asked.

"Um, there was a really long line. I'll stop on the way home."

Chapter Twenty-Four

~ Joanna ~

I got Mom and Dad a nurse to come in a few times a week to monitor his progress and track his pain medicines. I'd hired one only to make Mom feel better, but they probably didn't even need one for him. He was using crutches to move around and had to keep his leg elevated. Otherwise, he was actually fine.

Bathing would be tricky, but that was not something we'd asked the nurse to do. We got a shower chair and then Mom could simply help him get undressed and seated. If that didn't work, Stan said he was willing to help.

Friends, neighbors, and church had started an online sign-up to help with meals, so that was covered. Audrey and I could have easily handled that, but it was nice to have the love and support from the community. It had taken a huge weight off of trying to shop and prepare meals each day.

A few even took turns coming in to sit with Mom and visiting with Dad. It warmed my heart that people cared enough about my parents to pitch in.

We also hired a cleaning service to come in a few times a week to help out with the house and also a landscaping company to help with the yard. Unlike the nurse and meals from friends, this was a permanent solution, and it should keep my dad out of dangerous situations.

It probably was time for them to seriously start thinking about downsizing. Of course, there were several choices for 55+ apartments and townhouses, but I thought the community living would be nice for them, so I was going to suggest Birdsong Active Senior community. They were active people, and Birdsong had a lot of amenities.

From arts and crafts to various clubs to weekly movie nights. There was a pool and an exercise room. Both offered organized classes. There was a 9-hole putting green, a tennis court, and several gardens with walking trails.

Each unit had a kitchen, but Birdsong also had two cafeterias plus a coffee shop and deli.

You could keep your car, but they also provided a shuttle to go grocery shopping and once a week to the mall. Twice a week, they would provide transportation to a restaurant. It was by sign-up, and the restaurant changed each time.

Between their own kitchen, cafeterias, and the option to go to supper club, they had many options for meals. That would take a huge burden off of them.

I had a client several months ago that lived there. He had told me all about it, and I had looked into it briefly in case my parents ever hinted at downsizing. Now was time to pull this one out of my back pocket.

My phone rang.

"Hey, sis," I said, answering it.

"Hey. Are you going to Mom and Dad's?"

"Yeah, I was just loading up Oakley now."

"Be aware that Mom is in one of her moods. She isn't the center of attention and is desperately trying to be."

"Ugh, why?"

"Your guess is as good as mine."

Neither of us could ever answer this question. It was something we'd dealt with all of our lives. I told her I would report back after our visit.

"Alrighty, little Oakley, let's go see Grandma and Papa."

"G'an'ma. Papa." She giggled and kicked her little feet as I buckled her car seat.

We drove over, listening to her kid songs that she loved. I'd catch a word here or there as she sang along with all the songs.

While we were driving, a red sedan got on my tail, following me closely. They started to do the speed-up and slow-down thing that usually meant they were annoyed, so I moved over a lane. They changed lanes with me.

"Crap," I mumbled. It wasn't a random car. I was being followed for whatever reason. "Why now?"

I couldn't see in the car as the windows were tinted dark. It had paper tags and looked brand-new. Typically, this meant bad news for me. I slowed down a bit then took a right turn, and then the first left I could. They stayed right with me.

"Dang it."

Peeking in my mirror to the back seat, I hated that Oakley was with me. I had to be smart and think of how to handle this. I'd been followed before, and I liked to think I had gotten good at outrunning them.

I moved to a street with a lot of traffic lights and tried to maintain an even calm speed. Panicking wouldn't help, and it would tip off the other driver to what I was doing.

Unfortunately, we kept getting all the green lights. My plan of losing them at a light was not working.

I punched Clint's number on my car's display.

"Please answer," I mumbled as I listened to it ring.

"Hey, babe." When I heard his voice, I nearly broke down in tears.

"Clint... I have Oakley, and I'm being followed."

"Okay, okay, calm down." I heard him fumbling around on the other end, but his voice remained calm and steady. Just what I needed right now. "You've done this before, so you know it is normally intimidation or to track your movements. They rarely engage, right?"

"Right." I tried to remember if that had been my past experiences or not.

Yes, I think overall it was. Unless you counted when we moved from my home office to my new office building. We had been followed, and poor Al got shot. I wouldn't think about that now. I had to be calm for Oakley.

"Okay, so where are you?"

"I was heading to my parents but took a detour... Let's see... I'm on Laurel Drive close to downtown. Just passing Laurel Heights Park."

"Alright. You aren't far from Leo's. Drive there, and I'll call them to let them know you're heading that way. Maybe Eddie or Darius can meet you outside."

"Thanks."

"I'll call you back."

I maneuvered my car towards Leo's. A place that I was once scared of was now a place I ran to for safety.

My phone rang. This time it was Al.

"Hey, Al. Did Clint call you?"

"Yes, we're all here and ready for you."

"Okay, I'm two blocks away."

"Do you want me to stay on the phone with you?"

Before I could answer, the red car sped up next to me. The passenger window lowered an inch, and a gun appeared.

"Shit! A gun." I slammed on my brakes to try to put distance between us. The red car slowed, so I floored my car and took off towards Leo's as fast as possible.

Al talked the whole time, but I barely answered him as I focused on the other car. I wanted to keep distance between us. Thankfully Leo's came into sight.

"I can see you." He said. "Slow down."

Somehow, I turned into the lot at nearly full speed, or at least it felt like it. The red car paused, but they sped off when they saw Hank's men with guns at the ready.

Unlike last time, there was no gunfire, and it was a much better outcome when Al came to my side of the car.

"You okay?"

I looked back at Oakley, who was still singing away in the backseat, completely unaware of the danger we had just been in. Even with Mom's horrible driving, she didn't miss a beat.

"Yes." I sighed.

"Come in for a minute. Have a drink, and then I'll follow you home."

"Actually, I'm supposed to be at my parents'. You know how my mom gets."

He grimaced. "Okay, but come in for a few minutes in case that car circles back."

Clint messaged, and I replied that I was fine. I then messaged my mom that I would be a few minutes late then I shot off a message to Audrey letting her know exactly what happened. She told me to call her later.

Al carried Oakley in, and she babbled happily to her friend. She hadn't seen him in weeks, but they had a sweet, special relationship. Eddie came over and put his arms around my shoulders, guiding me in. I didn't mind, even after our awkward moment a few weeks ago when he asked me out.

Darius had a vodka cranberry in my hands before my eyes even adjusted to the dark interior.

"Ms. Joanna." Hank's deep voice came from behind. "I'm so glad you're okay. Any idea on that car?"

"None. Did Hacker get anything on the security tapes?"

"He's pulling it now to send over to the detectives."

"Thank you." I sipped the drink and watched as Oakley charmed the half-dozen guys that had surrounded us and come to our rescue once again. I owed them a lot. Maybe I would need to bake them some treats or do free readings.

"She reminds me of my daughter at that age," Matt said.

"I didn't know you have a daughter." I smiled at him.

"Yeah, she's twelve now. A daddy's girl. We went to the father-daughter dance at her school two weekends ago. She looked like a princess." He smiled as if thinking about her.

"Aw. I bet she did."

"Wanna see a picture?" He pulled out his phone.

"Oh, she's beautiful."

They didn't share their personal lives so I felt honored that he would share his daughter with me.

I continued to visit with the mob boss and his men for a few more minutes before thanking them and heading to my parents' house. Even though Hank sent Eddie to trail me over there, I still looked over my shoulder the entire way, and every car going in the same general direction posed a threat.

I finally pulled up at my family home.

Eddie pulled up next to me.

"Thanks, Eddie."

"Sure thing. Give me or any of us guys a call if you want us to come to escort you home." He winked.

"I will." I said, turning my face so he didn't see me blush.

I watched him drive away as I unloaded Oakley, then turned towards my childhood home. The place I'd grown up and for a moment hated the thought of them selling the house and moving, though I knew it was the right decision, or at least I was going to try to convince them that it was.

Going into the familiar front door of the house, stepping into the dated foyer with its green and mustard colored floral wallpaper that had seen better days had me remembering all the times coming through this door. The memories flooded my mind.

I walked from there through the square wood grain doorway into the dark and dated living room where I found my father laid up with a foot-to-nearly-hip cast.

Seeing him laid up, I knew they'd need to move to keep him off the roof. Of course, I had already taken steps to help that, but the final one would be getting them into a much different living situation.

I leaned over to kiss his head and then sat in a nearby chair. My mother scooped up Oakley, and they were having a private conversation in the kitchen with a cookie.

"How are you feeling today?"

"A little better. Not feeling the pain as much, but it's there. The pain medicine helps." He chuckled.

"That's good. The cleaning service and homecare are all working out?"

"It is. Thank you for that. It really takes the burden off of us."

"So, have y'all heard of Birdsong Senior Living Community?"

"We aren't ready for a nursing home." My father said. "It's just a broken leg."

"It's not a nursing home. It's a 55+ community. They have many amenities like cafeterias, clubs, swimming pool. The apartments come in one or two bedrooms. They have some that even have an extra room for an office or crafts."

"I don't know, Joanna. That sounds expensive." My mother said from the other room.

"There are other places, but I thought this one sounded like it could be a good fit for the two of you."

"How do you know so much about it?" she asked as she and Oakley joined us in the living room. She passed the baby a couple of toys.

"I had a client that lives there. He told me about it, and it really sounds like a nice community. Also Laney's grandmother lives there. She seems happy."

"We have wonderful friends and neighbors here. Have you seen how much food they have been dropping off?" My dad said. "We had to ask them to slow down because we would never eat that much."

"Can you both just think about it? Look at it online or take a tour. And as I said, there are other places, but most don't have the activities and things that Birdsong has."

"Fine. We'll look." Dad said.

"That's all I'm asking. I love you both and just want you to be safe and happy."

"We are." Mom said.

When I got home, I called Audrey and filled her in on my afternoon, especially the car following and shooting at me.

"Jo, that's scary."

"Very especially since I have no idea why or who they were."

"Do you think it could be those weird Crawfords? You said they were at the hospital the other day."

"Maybe. I hadn't thought of them." They had seemed at least civil when we parted ways the other day, but who knows? They had a reputation for hot tempers and snarky comebacks. "I have also run into those guys that attacked Percy."

"What? When?"

"Once on the way to the hospital to visit Percy and then again at Brights."

"Jo, that's really scary. Have you told Clint or Hank?"

"Only you so far."

"You need to tell Clint at least."

"Okay."

But I knew I wouldn't. He would be angry, and I couldn't handle that. So far, the guys hadn't really done anything to me. It seemed more like a scare tactic. Unless they were the same guys in the car. I'd just be careful and be more aware of my surroundings.

"How did Mom seem while you were there?"

"Oh, she seemed okay, but probably because I had Oakley."

"True. She acts okay around Harris and Dylan too." She chuckled. "We get the crazy side of her."

"I talked to them about downsizing, and they seemed open."

"Oh, good. That would be one less thing for us to worry about with them."

"Yes. Well, that's it. I'll let you go for now. Love you, sis."

"Love you more, little sis."

Chapter Twenty-Five

~ Joanna ~

My appointments were back to being fully booked. Whatever weird blip in my business happened, it seemed to be over, at least for now. I was going to put that other medium out of my mind as much as possible.

I checked over my schedule for the day and one of the names caught my attention. Vera Beckett. Stepdaughter to Senator Crawford.

"What does she want?" I muttered and then walked out to the reception area to talk to Tessa.

Thankfully there weren't any clients yet, and Vera's appointment was this afternoon, so I had all day to stew and process this and hopefully get Arnie or Hedy here as a backup.

Sadly, since I had no cell phone to the dead and my past attempts to conjure spirits had failed miserably, I'd have to wait and hope one showed up.

"Vera made an appointment?" I asked when I got to the reception desk. I hadn't forgotten New Year's at Brights.

"Yeah, I tried to put her off, but she was persistent." Tessa said. "I know you can handle whatever she throws at you."

"She'll probably try to live stream it like she does her entire life." I groaned and leaned against the reception desk counter.

That is what Vera Beckett did for a living. People gave her clothing, makeup, even food to try and talk about. If it could be marketed, people asked Vera. I have to admit that I've watched more than my fair share of Vera Vibes, and of course, I tried to do some of those dances a few weeks ago. Unfortunately, that had been a miserable fail.

"Are you going to let her?"

"Maybe. I don't know how I could stop her." I paused, looking around at the different spirits in the room. "I'm just worried as I haven't spoken to Arnie or Hedy in... a while. If one of them doesn't show up, what will I do?"

"Fake it?"

"I guess I could. I know enough about the Crawford family, especially now, to say a few things, and I have some time to research." I paused to collect my thoughts. "But I don't want to fake it ever again. Now that I have been doing this for real, I hate that I had deceived people all those years. I'm a medium with a heart for a reason."

"You're a good person, Jo, don't forget that." She stood and reached out for my hand. "You were giving people love and happiness in a time of grief. If that isn't heart, then I don't know what is."

"Aw, Tessa, you're such a good friend." I blew her a kiss and went to the back to prepare for my first client.

The morning flew by, and before long, it was lunchtime, which I was skipping so I could research more about Vera. I jotted down a few mental notes about her and her life. I'm sure she wanted to know about Arnie and his heir, but I would steer the conversation to anything but that.

"Um, hello?" A deep voice at the door said.

"Arnie! I'm so happy to see you. Where have you been?"

"I've been just wandering around. I hung around Hank for a bit then just aimlessly." He sighed. "This all seems so hopeless right now. Even with what you told me about my autopsy, there isn't much else out there or way to find the killer."

"I'm sorry."

I didn't have anything better to say because it really did seem hopeless. Unless Hank changed his mind, the inheritance would go to people that could have killed Arnie. Unfortunately, we were down to a little over a month to the deadline, and Hank didn't seem anywhere close to changing his mind.

He simply shrugged in reply.

"Did you hear that Vera is coming in shortly?"

"No, I guess it's a good thing I came by then." He chuckled.

"Yes, I'm so thankful you did." Then I realized something. "Why are you here?"

"I was going to thank you for trying and that I'm going to just forget the whole thing."

"No, I know there is something here. I don't know what, but something. Oh, and hey, I think my boyfriend, remember the detective, he is actively working on your case. He mentioned something about going to Centerville soon, and though he was vague about the details, I think it has to do with you."

"Really? Well, that is a development."

"Yeah, but he didn't tell me much, probably so I didn't do anything stupid," I said absently.

"Is that a habit of yours?" Arnie asked.

"Sadly, yes. I get so wrapped up in these things and then forget it can be dangerous."

"Um, yeah, I can see it."

I didn't have time to react or let the insult sink in because at that moment, Tessa buzzed my phone to say the circus had arrived.

"Vera's here," I said as I hung up the phone.

"Let's get to it." He said.

Taking a deep breath, I steadied myself for the craziness I was about to endure and as I walked to the reception, my heart was nearly beating out of my chest. I knew I could handle this, but I simply didn't want to deal with Vera. She was a lot of person in a little body and my past experience with her was still fresh in my mind.

"Well, here we are, my fans! I'm about to get a reading with famed medium, Joanna Webber..." I could hear her talking before I opened the door. I took a deep breath and then pushed through the door. "And here she is now!"

"Hi," I said to the cell phone that had been thrust in my face. I couldn't see much, but a lot of words scrolling which I assumed were comments to her live stream. "I'm surprised you made an appointment. I thought you didn't believe in me."

"Oh, I don't, but I thought I'd come anyway. It's good for my brand. Oh, mikeymuscles, you're so bad, but you ain't lyin'." She giggled as she read the comments from viewers. "So, lead the way, let's get this reading started... though I expect this to be faaake!"

"If she was a fake, would she be able to tell you about the time I found you with green hair when you tried coloring it yourself? I discreetly drove you to the hair salon, so they could help fix it." I repeated Arnie's words. I wish I could have high-fived him for the best story.

"What? How do you know that?" She dropped her arm with the phone in it to her side.

"Or would she know about the time when you were 13 and got into my liquor cabinet? You were so drunk that you got sick. I helped you get cleaned up and into bed before your mother found out."

"Arnie?" She mumbled. Tears formed in her eyes. "I've missed you so much."

Her phone made a sound. She mumbled as she tapped a couple of buttons and then dropped it into her purse.

"You do?" He asked.

"Yes, I didn't realize until I saw you lying there... you were a better father to me than my own."

She honestly sounded sincere. Her 180-degree personality shift had me reconsidering my impression of her a bit. Maybe she was just a lost kid who was grieving like so many of us, fighting our own battles.

"I didn't know you felt that way." I said for Arnie, and then I suggested, "Why don't we take this back to the reading room?"

She nodded and followed me.

"Okay, now let's continue here in private." I looked to both Arnie and Vera. She was staring, her eyes glassy and watery. I passed her a box of tissues. She flashed a weak smile.

"I'm so sorry for being such a brat all those years."

"You were just a kid. I didn't take it personally."

She laughed. "You were always so nice and understanding. So, do you know what happened to you? I always thought of you as this larger than life... my hero so many times, and here you were... dying on the floor." She choked the last words out.

"Oh, Vera, I didn't know you felt that way about me. I thought you hated me."

"Well, yeah, I mean in a way, like spoiled teens hate their parents, but I loved you too. You were the only parent that seemed to care about me. If I tried to talk to my mother, she just bought me stuff. And my dad, well, you know, was not around at all. He started that new family and left us completely." She grabbed a few tissues, dabbing her eyes.

"I loved you too as if you were my own, and I only wanted the best for you."

"So, what happened that day? Do you know how you died?"

"I don't... I remember I went jogging that morning. After that, I worked in my office on a new bill I was hoping to propose, and then I went to lunch with... a friend. After lunch, I had my usual afternoon drink, and then that's it."

There was something about how he paused on the who he had lunch with part. Was that the person? Or was it a lady, and he didn't want Vera to know? That had to be it. I remember him saying he had started talking to a lawyer about divorcing Irene.

"Well, I miss you, and I love you." Vera choked out.

"I miss you and love you too, baby girl," Arnie said.

"So, would you tell me who this heir is? I would love to have this all behind us." She said sweetly.

"I can't. He still has time to claim the money and deserves the time to process this and come forward."

Vera's body suddenly tensed up. "That's not fair. You should tell me... Wait? Was that really Arnie, or are you making all this up?"

"Vera, it's really me. Do you need another memory? How about when I took you to buy that dress you wanted for homecoming. The hot pink one that your mother said you couldn't have because you had gotten a C in English. I bought it for you and took the wrath. You got voted homecoming queen."

She eyed me. "You couldn't have known that unless he told you. Fine. Fine, but Arnie, I don't understand why you can't tell me. I just want to talk to him and ask that he not change my allowance. I can't lose my status. I'm an icon and a role model to so many, but I can't keep this up without my allowance."

She probably really believed that, and maybe it was true, but she wasn't the type of role model I would want Oakley to look up to. Beauty and fame weren't everything. Hard work, kindness, and being a good person were what I valued, and I hoped that Oakley would have similar values.

"And that's our time for today. I hope this was helpful to you."

"Don't think that I have changed my feelings about you, Joanna. Just because you got lucky with this... you're still ruining my life by not telling us who this heir is. For all I know, Arnie is telling you, and you're just picking and choosing what to tell me. Just enough to be believable without giving anything away."

"Well, you'll just have to make up your own mind to believe or not. Remember you came to me." I stood and gestured for her to do the same.

We walked in silence out to the reception area.

"Thank you, and Tessa will finalize your visit." I turned sharply and returned to my office. I wanted this entire visit out of my head. I was emotionally drained by her energy and this reading in general.

Arnie was following me around, and I really wanted to ignore him.

"I'm sorry, Arnie, I am so exhausted. Is there anything else I can do for you now?"

"I guess not. I just want to thank you for that. I didn't know she thought of me that way."

"Yeah, that was probably good to hear."

"It was." He stood there as if not wanting to leave but didn't continue to speak.

I took a seat at my desk and pulled up emails. It might seem rude, but I was mentally and emotionally drained from their reading. Vera's energy was enough to zap it out of me but them together was a lot to handle.

To some, it might seem simple, a conversation between two people that loved each other, but there was so much at stake. And the fact she keeps turning on me is just not something I want to deal with today.

"I guess I'll leave. I really appreciate your time."

I smiled and nodded but didn't say anything. I continued reading my emails and didn't look up again until he was gone.

Once he was, I just laid my head on my desk and cried. Cried from the overwhelming feelings I felt for them, for myself, and just to cleanse my stress level. I hated the negative readings. Even when there was some positive, it felt like it had ended on a sour note. He wouldn't give up who the heir was, and she still hated me, though I cared less about that part.

After my cry, I wiped my face and gathered myself up. Thankfully it was my last appointment so I wouldn't have to deal with another client. I could simply head home and snuggle with my baby and my dog.

Chapter Twenty-Six

~ Joanna ~

"Alright, Beatrice, any more words for Edgar?" I was doing a reading for a lovely couple and their adult children.

"I just want to thank you for the 55 years you stood by my side and loved me. I miss you daily." She wiped her eyes. Her daughter, Joan, reached over to hold her mother's hand.

"Oh, darlin', it was my pleasure. You were the best parts of my life, and I will be by your side as long as I can." I said for him.

"And, Daddy," Joan said, "I will keep your memory alive for my children. They all miss you so much."

"Aw, that means so much. I miss them too and will be watching over all of you."

We wrapped up with that, and I walked them to the lobby.

"Can I give you a hug?" Beatrice asked.

"Of course." I put my arms out, and we embraced.

"Thank you so much for all you do. It really helps in my grief."

"It is what I was born to do."

Then Joan hugged me, thanking me for my time.

"It was my pleasure. Anytime you want to return, just give us a call."

I nodded to Edgar, who was standing right next to Beatrice. He smiled and then looked at his bride.

I love the happy readings. Instead of draining my energy, they pump me up. Seeing the people smiling, crying joyful tears, and sharing happy memories.

There weren't hidden agendas or hurt feelings, like there had been with all the Crawfords. I would be so thankful when this was solved, and they were out of my life.

But I wouldn't focus on that now. I would embrace the high of my positive readings.

With that reading complete, I would need to get set up for my next and that meant cleaning up the reading room and prepping it for the next appointment. When I reached the room, I took a moment to simply admire it. It was my favorite room. I found peace when I was in here.

The furniture was carefully selected for its comfort and softness with light-colored fabric. The artwork was floral abstracts in soft blues, greens, and yellows on white backgrounds. They complemented the sofa and side chairs well. Instead of using harsh overhead lighting, I had lamps in the room.

I did my typical wiping everything down, emptying the trash, setting out fresh drinks and tissues, and fluffing the cushions and pillows. Then stood back once more to admire my beautiful room.

Checking the time, I had a few minutes before the next appointment, so I grabbed a fresh cup of coffee and then went to check my emails and my cell phone.

But, walking into my office, I was met with a surprise visitor.

"Oh, um, Irene, how...? What?"

Like the last time, she was sitting at my desk as if it was her office. She was scrolling through her phone, but as I came in, she gestured for me to have a seat in the guest chair. Again, this was my office, and yet again, I was being ordered where to sit. Her confident stare had me not questioning her.

"Ah, finally. I have been waiting for you to finish up. That was lengthy."

"That's my job." I said firmly and trying to sound confident. "What can I help you with?"

"I heard what happened with Vera yesterday."

"What do you mean?" Nothing much had happened, at least not with her visit, but at the club a few weeks ago, now that was something.

"Just that she came here and started a live stream. She really needs to stop."

"Oh, it wasn't so bad." I smiled, trying to fake my confidence. "I think she was happy with the results of the reading."

"You were able to do one with her?"

"Yes, didn't she tell you?"

"No, we don't talk much these days. She hates me." She frowned. "Who was it with? Arnie?"

"It was actually. They had a nice conversation, but I should leave her to tell you details."

"Is he here now? I miss him." She looked around.

"Really?"

"Yes, why are you so surprised? I was married to him." She sighed. "Sure we had issues, what couples don't? And yes, at times, it was more of a business deal, but... I loved him." Irene's face fell.

"You did love him, huh?"

"Again, why are you so surprised?" Her body tensed.

"I just didn't know." I paused. She didn't speak, so I continued. "He may have said that you didn't have the best marriage, and I hate to say, but you have a... reputation."

She cleared her throat and straightened in the chair. "Well, be that as it may, I loved him in my own way. It doesn't matter now, and besides, I knew he was speaking with a lawyer before he died."

"I'm sorry." I didn't mention that he'd already told me that, so it wasn't a surprise to hear her say it. Though at her confession, I did feel bad for her.

"It's not your problem. I just wish I could tell him that for what it's worth, I did love him and enjoyed our years together."

"If he were around, I would happily do a reading, and next time he comes by, I will ask him, and we can figure out a time for you two to connect. I'm sure he would do it."

"You think he would? I would like that. Thank you." She stood but then plopped back down with a sigh. "I still wanted to apologize for Vera."

"Okay."

"I feel like I've failed her in so many ways. She's so caught up in this social media stuff with all the likes and comments. She's obsessed and does whatever it takes to get them. Like coming in here or what she pulled at Brights on New Year's. It's her life now, and not anything personal to you."

"I don't know what to say but thank you?" I was confused by her attempt at an apology, but now I had confirmation that she knew about that night. I had wondered.

"You have a child, right? That one you adopted."

"Yes." She already knew that, not sure where she was going with her thoughts here.

"Don't let her get caught up in all this social media business or really anything online." She looked at me and then tossed her hands up. "It's such a difficult time to parent. All the technology and whatnot, then balancing between letting them experience life and do things like their friends, while keeping them safe."

"I'll remember that." I smiled politely.

She flashed a faint smile. "I'm just worried that Vera has gotten wrapped up in some stuff and has been hanging around some bad people. There are always these boys with her. They do anything she says. If she says jump, they don't even ask how high. They just jump."

"I think everyone gets bad friends at some point." Didn't Irene have friends to vent to? Why did she think I wanted to hear this?

She was quiet for a moment before standing again. "Well, I've taken up enough of your time. I'll see you at the Harper's Angels Event Friday, right?"

"Yes, I'll be there."

"Wonderful." She started to walk out, but then stopped at the doorway. "I don't feel like just saying it is enough. Let me make this up to you. Why don't you come by the house tomorrow for lunch? Around noon?"

I stared at her for a moment. How could I get out of this? Why was she asking me to her house and not a restaurant? She was suspected of murder, and if it was her, should I be worried?

In the end, as it usually did, curiosity won out.

"I'll be there. Thank you."

"Great." She walked over and wrote down her address. "I'll have your name on the guest list at the gate. See you then." With that she disappeared.

I may never know how she got in here without being seen or why she was telling me her worries about her daughter, but as long as she felt better about things, that was good enough for me.

Now to worry about the true reason she wanted me at her house. It could be to eat finger sandwiches and salad, or whatever rich people ate for lunch, but more likely she hoped to connect with Arnie.

I couldn't decide if I wanted him to or not. It could get awkward, especially if she talked about her feelings or asked about the heir. Honestly, any conversation with Irene was going to be uncomfortable.

I laid my head on my desk and then realized I was still sitting in the guest chair.

"That woman." I stood and walked around to my desk chair, but by then my coffee was cold. "That woman." I muttered again.

I headed to the breakroom to pour out this cup. As I watched the caramel-colored liquid swirl down the drain, I thought again about Arnie.

He had led such a lonely life and missed out on his son's entire life. It was clear he had loved Hank and wanted to be involved, he just let life move around him.

He regretted and had remorse. I loved that he'd gotten some closure with Vera, so maybe it would be good to get that with Irene.

"Fine. I'll go."

"Go where, boss." Micah said.

"Oh, hi. Um, Irene asked me to lunch tomorrow at her house."

"Wow, that's... interesting."

"Yeah, my thoughts exactly."

"And so, you're going?"

"Yep."

"I assume the invite didn't include a plus one?"

"Right, and I'm sure she wouldn't appreciate an extra guest."

"Well, please promise you'll be cautious and text me when you get there and then once you leave." He wrapped his arms around me. "Love you, friend."

I was so glad to have met him all those years ago. He truly was one of my best friends.

"I love you too."

Chapter Twenty-Seven

~ Joanna ~

I stood in front of my closet with Oakley playing at my feet. I was dropping her off with Auntie Tessa on my way out to Centerville and this dreaded lunch with Irene.

"What to wear, what to wear?" I flipped through my tops. "Not this one. Blah, not that one."

I had no idea what to wear to lunch with a potential killer in her highly elite mansion. She said it was an apology for her daughter's behavior towards me, but I couldn't shake the feeling it was more.

Checking the time, I realized I was running out of time if I was going to drive the baby to Tessa's and then make the near hour-long drive over to Centerville. It wasn't far, but with traffic between the cities, it could cause me to be late. I got the impression that would piss Irene off big time.

I pulled out some charcoal gray slacks and a navy-blue pinstripe blouse. Over the blouse, I pulled on a dark red sweater, then adjusted the blouse under it so that the collar was straight and neat, and the tail of the blouse at the bottom of the sweater so it didn't bunch up.

Then I dug out my favorite red flats. I'd gotten lucky when I'd found these because they matched my sweater almost perfectly.

Finally, I added a silver chain necklace that had several thin long strands. It was delicate and classy.

"So, what do you think?" I modeled for Oakley.

"Ma. Ma." She clapped.

"I take it you approve."

I quickly pulled my hair into a neat bun, brushed on a little mascara, and applied a touch of tinted lip gloss.

Once I was ready, I gathered up Oakley and her things that Tessa would need. Bag packed, baby changed, and I was dressed.

"No more stalling." I chastised myself as I picked up the bag and baby, then headed to my car.

Driving to Tessa's, I watched over my shoulder as I had gotten in the habit of doing. Nothing seemed sketchy but I was extra paranoid today. Irene was still number one on my suspect list, but I was leaving most of the sleuthing to Clint this time.

Also, I realized I hadn't told him about going to Irene's. He probably wouldn't like it, but thankfully, he was so caught up in his investigation that he shouldn't even know. Unless this went sideways, there was no reason for him to ever know or find out.

As I pulled up at Tessa's house, she was outside waiting for me, along with her sister, Elsa.

"Oh, hey, Elsa. I didn't know you were still home." I said, stepping out of my car. "When do you head back to college?"

I moved to the back door to unbuckle Oakley.

"It was supposed to be today, but I couldn't miss out on seeing this little one." She held her arms out for Oakley who leapt to her with a giggle. "Aw, hi, sweetie-pie. Let's go in and play. I got some fun toys for you to play with."

Then Elsa carried her into the house while my daughter babbled and giggled. I didn't even get to say goodbye, but I'd only be gone a few hours, hopefully.

"You gonna be okay going to Irene's alone?" Tessa asked as I handed her the diaper bag.

"Yeah, it'll be fine. I'm sure she just wants to talk and probably hopes I'll bring Arnie with me."

"Is he with you?"

"Sadly, no and I haven't talked to him, so he technically doesn't know about this. Unless he heard it through the ghost-vine."

"The what?"

"Just something I heard once from a spirit. Like hearing a rumor through the grapevine."

She laughed. "Ah, clever."

"Well, thank you for watching her. I should probably be going. Never know about traffic."

She stepped forward and hugged me. "Be safe."

"I will."

With that, I pointed my car towards Centerville. I didn't even bother with looking over my shoulder this time, I was too nervous about this lunch. I needed Arnie or even Hedy. Someone from the other side that had knowledge of the family history.

"Come on, please hear me." I mumbled.

When I finally reached Irene's gated community, I turned down the radio. It was only then that I realized in my distracted state, I'd never changed the radio from Oakley's music.

"Well, that could have been embarrassing." I said, just before pulling up to give the guard my name.

"Joanna Webber?" He repeated.

"Yes, that's right."

He scanned his list and then tapped his finger on it. "Yes, right here. Irene Crawford." Then he looked up at me. "Wait, you're that medium?"

"I am." I smiled my best Joanna medium with a heart smile for him.

"I have always wanted to meet you, but I didn't have the nerve to make an appointment with you." He looked around. "Is there anyone here with me?"

I looked to his right at the older woman. "There is. Your mother, Terry. She says she's so proud of you."

He looked to his right. "Mom. I've missed you."

"She says you should call your father. He worries about you and would love an update. You have so much good happening with your life now."

His eyes went wide. "Wow. Okay, I'll call him as soon as I get off of work."

I nodded towards the gate arm that was still in my way. He jumped and pushed the button to raise it.

"I hope that the message makes you feel better. If you call my office, tell Tessa you are the security guard here and I said you can have a free reading, anytime."

"Thank you. That's so generous."

I had to remember to tell Tessa about this. I'd need to come up with a code word to use or something.

I drove around the neighborhood of homes I could never imagine owning. They were gorgeous and huge. What did they do with all that space?

Personally, I liked my quaint home with just enough space for my daughter, my goofy mutt, and me, and maybe even a certain guy.

I then pulled in front of the Crawford mansion, a white stucco with clean lines and very little personality. It was stunning and modern but lacked the character of my own neighborhood. There were no kids playing or people watering their lawns.

I approached the ornate front door and rang the bell.

"I'm coming." Irene said through her doorbell camera.

After a moment, I could hear her heels clicking as she approached the door. It flew open. "Welcome to my home. I'm so glad you came." She waved for me to come in.

"Thank you."

I stepped into the most gorgeous yet sterile foyer I'd ever seen. The ceiling was easily 20 or more feet tall with an intricate glass sculptured light fixture. The floors were wide white tiles, and the entire thing was void of anything personal, like a family picture or shoes or anything that gave a clue to the people who lived here.

"I thought we'd eat on the back porch." She gestured for me to follow her.

We walked through the massive house. I tried to have a look around so I could understand her a bit, but just as in the foyer, there were no clues. Not a picture of her children, of Arnie, of a beloved puppy. Nothing to give me an idea of what this woman liked.

We stepped out the back door to the patio where she had set up an elegant spread. It looked more like she had prepared for a bridal shower, not lunch with an acquaintance.

The table was dressed in a crisp white tablecloth and sage green cloth napkins tied with twine and set on the sage green plates. The centerpiece was made of pale pink roses, tiny white flowers, and wide, waxy greenery.

"Wow, Irene, this is lovely."

"Thank you." She gestured for me to sit. "I hope you like chicken salad."

"I do."

"I have croissants, sourdough, or lettuce if you prefer." She smiled as she plucked a croissant from the stack. "The croissants are my favorite. I get them from this bakery downtown."

"They look good." I took one and followed her lead filling it with chicken salad. Then I added a spoonful of fruit salad to my plate. "Thank you for inviting me."

"Well, I really wanted to apologize for Vera."

"Why should you apologize for me?" Vera said, stepping outside. I think this was the first time I had seen her not holding her phone doing a live stream.

"Oh, Vera, I didn't know you were home." Irene said.

"I wasn't. I just got here." She glared at me. "What is she doing here? And don't say you are apologizing for me. If I was sorry, I would do it myself."

"Vera, that is extremely rude. You need to apologize to our guest."

"She's not my guest and you said you asked her to make up for my bad attitude or whatever. You can tell her sorry for this too." She grabbed a croissant and went back inside, slamming the door behind her.

"See what I mean? She's out of control. I didn't raise her to act like that."

Before I could reply, I heard a familiar voice call my name. "Joanna?"

I looked over to see Arnie. "Arnie, what are you doing here?"

"Arnie's here?" Irene said, looking around wildly.

"I've been following Vera around a little bit. We just went shoe shopping. It was boring, but now that I know how she feels about me, it felt good to watch over her."

"Is it really him? Did he say anything?" Irene asked, her hands clasped together.

"You might as well tell her that I am." He said flatly as he crossed his arms over his chest.

"Yes, he is." I pointed towards the back door.

She spun around to face the door. "Oh, Arnie, I'm so glad you're here. I've missed you."

"You have?" As usual, I tried to deliver his words with the feeling he intended and as usual, I likely failed.

"Of course, why wouldn't I?"

"We didn't have the best relationship and when I was alive, you could barely be in the same room with me."

"That's not... okay, fine, but I was just mad at you. You worked all the time and rarely had time for me. I craved attention."

"I gave you attention."

"Only in front of people, that's why I always wanted to host dinner parties." She smiled. "Plus I'm really good at it."

"Well, I think this spread you set up for lunch is wonderful. Thank you."

They both stared at me. Clearly my job here was just to translate his messages. Message received.

"Sorry, I'll get back to passing his messages." I listened to Arnie. "He does agree that you were a wonderful host."

She smiled and blushed slightly. I guess that was a point of pride for her and I could tell by the care she had put into our simple lunch that she took it seriously.

"I really tried to make you proud of me. I know I wasn't perfect, and I know that I was just a trophy wife to you, but I loved you."

"Oh, Irene, I loved you too." He sighed. "We just had a different type of marriage than some."

Tears formed in her eyes. "That's all I can ask for. Thank you."

We all sat in silence. I eyed the chicken salad croissant waiting for me to eat it, but I knew it would be rude to continue with lunch until they were done. I just didn't know when that was going to be.

"Did you have anything else to say to me?" Irene finally asked.

"Such as?"

"Such as who this heir is and what am I supposed to do without you now? I've just been floundering around trying to find myself."

"Do whatever you want. You have your whole life ahead of you and a ton of money to boot. And no, I'm not going to tell you my son's name. He doesn't want to come forward, so you'll likely be fine."

"I'm so sorry to hear that. As a mother, I can't imagine if my children didn't want anything to do with me."

He stared at her, mouth open and eyes wide. I guess that isn't what he thought he'd hear.

"You understand?"

"I do. I know my reputation is... well a bitch, but frankly, I have a soft spot when it comes to my children and from what I understand of your story, you had a son out of wedlock and never got to be in his life. Am I right?"

"You are. You know the expectations when it comes to being a Crawford. I had to deny him which broke my heart, but it was the only thing I knew to do at the time."

"Yes, and I'm sorry you and he didn't get to have a relationship. I'm trying desperately to hold on to a relationship with my two. Dodge is mostly quiet, and I never see him. He spends most of his time playing video games and creating videos about gaming." She sighed and tears formed in her eyes. "Then Vera, oh, Vera is lost in this online world too, but she seems so much more obsessed than Dodge, and honestly, I'm scared for her."

"I followed her around today and other than her obsession with putting nearly her every move online, she seemed okay."

"Really? Do you think I'm being paranoid?"

"Yeah, she's fine. She'll be fine."

"Okay, good. Thank you." She dabbed at her eyes. "I'm so glad to talk to you again, even if it is through Joanna." She smiled at me. "Thank you."

"I hope it helps." He said. "Well, I'll let you ladies get back to your lunch. I didn't mean to interrupt."

"I'm so glad you stopped by. I miss you."

He nodded and was gone.

"He's gone now." I said, looking at the wall where he disappeared.

"Oh, Joanna, I'm so thankful for you. That's all I ever wanted was to talk to him once more, especially about Vera. They had a special bond, even if she tried to act all tough and like she hated him. In her way, she loved him and needed him."

"I'm glad I was able to finally give you that."

"Well, let's eat!" She giggled. I could feel her weight had been lifted and was the first time I ever felt relaxed around her.

With that behind us, I finally got to eat this amazing croissant, and it was worth the wait.

"Irene, you were right. This is one of the best croissants."

"Well, save room. I have tiny bundt cakes from the same shop. They are lemon raspberry and are to die for."

"Sounds wonderful."

An hour later, with our visit coming to a close, my impression of her had changed drastically and wiped out my negative thoughts from our previous encounters. We shared stories of our children. She was a loving, caring mother.

"Thank you for inviting me, Irene. I really enjoyed it." I said at the doorway as I prepared to leave.

"No, thank you. I'm so glad you were able to do the reading with Arnie. Finally. Oh, and I'm so sorry for calling you a fake." She leaned towards me for a hug.

Earlier today, I would never have thought this possible, but all it took was closure. Like so many that are grieving, she had just needed those few words to feel better.

I messaged both Tessa and Micah that I was done and heading back to Creekview. Since I was safe, at least at the moment, there was no reason to let Clint know I'd ever been out here.

Chapter Twenty-Eight

~ Clint ~

Today, Terry and I were heading over to the Senator's former residence where his wife and stepchildren still lived to execute the search warrants that I'd finally been able to secure.

We had additional teams going to the Meyers-Crawford home and the estate of Oren and Viola Crawford. We needed to hit them all quickly and at once.

We were partnering with the Centerville department, as it was out of our jurisdiction, which had added a whole new level of difficulty to get all of this executed. Still, once I'd proven this was worth their time, they reopened the case.

It had taken a lot of research for me to determine if I could show probable cause, which, thanks to Freddy's secret autopsy, had made that piece a lot easier. Then I had to determine if the items were even still there, but through luck and skills, and maybe a few favors, including some Hank called in, we had the documents we needed to move forward.

I couldn't wait to see how this played out. If everything fell into place, I would have the final proof I needed to believe this whole medium business and also prove to myself that I was a great detective after all. Unfortunately, my self-esteem had taken a real hit over the past couple of months.

"And you're sure that she still has his computer, cell phone, and this security footage?"

"It was there at his death, and the CPD didn't take it when he died. From my investigation, she had tried to sell the items but couldn't or maybe changed her mind. I don't know."

"Maybe when she heard about his will, she thought it might have clues on it?"

"Yes, maybe so." Which is precisely what I had banked on when I got the information about her trying to but not selling the items.

We got to the security gate for their neighborhood and identified ourselves. After verifying us, they waved us through.

"Some swanky homes." Terry whistled as we drove through.

"I'm not a fan of these mini mansions. They are so cookie cutter."

"True."

But I had to admit I was curious to get a peek inside a few of these. How did they fill them up, and were there rooms they just never went into?

My home was a small ranch with 3 bedrooms, one bathroom, and roughly 1,200 square feet. Perfect for my bachelor's lifestyle. I thought briefly of Joanna's new home. It was approximately 800 square feet bigger and would be just the right size for our family.

I smiled at the thought, and then shook it off to focus on the case as we were nearly there.

A moment later, we pulled up in front of the Crawford home. It was modern in design with straight lines and picture windows. Stark white stucco and black metal framed the door and windows. Nothing screamed welcome home to me, but that was just my simple tastes. I guess this did appeal to others and who was I to judge that?

Terry and I parked at the curb, and the others parked behind us. They waited while Terry and I approached the door to serve the search warrants.

"Well, hello, officers." Irene Crawford greeted us at the door. A fluted cocktail glass in hand, dressed in a bikini in January. "You caught me just about to hit my tanning bed. May I ask why you are here today?"

"Yes, ma'am. We have a warrant for all computers, cell phones, phone records, and security footage from the weeks leading up to and after the Senator's death. We have the exact dates listed here in the warrant." Terry pointed to them.

"I see. Well, I'll gladly give you all of Arnie's things and even mine, but you will be hard-pressed to get them from my children."

She offered it as a challenge but didn't seem all that surprised to see us or that we were asking about this nearly two years after his death. I took a mental note of her reaction.

"Well, ma'am, it's the law. They will have to give them up to us. If we find nothing on them, they can be returned, but these things take time to process. So, you may just want to purchase new cell phones." Terry offered.

Irene simply laughed but stepped aside for us to enter. I signaled for the other officers, and we began the process of bagging and tagging everything.

"Mother! This is not fair. Not fair at all. My cell phone is my life. You know that!" Vera screeched. "Y'all are out to get me! All of you. Out to get me!"

She screamed and stomped and screamed more, but in the end, handed over the phone.

Dodge had been quieter in his protest but was clearly not thrilled with this invasion. After we had possession of his things, he slammed his door so hard the art on nearby walls shook.

Irene just sipped her drink and stared daggers through us as we worked. On occasion, she would tap her toe with impatience.

The head of her security team brought us a USB drive. "It's not of the moment of death. We were doing, um, maintenance that day, but it's the week leading up to and a week after his death, as requested."

"Thank you," I said, taking it and noting it as evidence.

"Not sure what you are hoping to do with all this. He died of a heart attack." He said.

"And, how would you know that without an autopsy?" We hadn't made it public that we had one yet.

His eyes widened at my statement. Perhaps he hadn't known that bit of detail.

"That's how it was reported on his death certificate, so I just assumed that an autopsy was done."

"Unfortunately, no, but thank you for this. It will be helpful."

I walked through the Senator's office to see if there were any clues that I had missed. On his desk was his day planner. I didn't know people still used these, opting for technology to track appointments and things, but then he was old school, so it made sense. I glanced around and then down at it, but I couldn't do anything else with it as it wasn't on the search warrant.

I was surprised to see that it was still opened to the day before and the day of his death. The only things on the pages were a physical the day before and a lunch appointment with the letters HH on the day of his death. I made a mental note of those two things, but I didn't know if they would mean anything.

We spent several hours gathering everything, but finally we were packed up and ready to head back to Centerville Police Department.

"I hope you find whatever it is that you think you will find here, officers, but honestly, you're barking up the wrong tree," Irene said at the doorway, still in her bikini and sipping a cocktail.

"Thank you for your cooperation today. We'll let you know when you may have your belongings back."

She cackled before slamming the door behind us. I guess we knew how she felt about our invasion.

"Yikes," Terry said as we got in the car. "I'm glad that's over."

"Me too."

"Remind me what you hope to find on this?"

"Clues. Any clues. Ones that can lead us to the killer or how those drugs were purchased, or even who else we should look at. Anything. Something."

"You believe Joanna now?"

I looked at him for a moment, thinking about his question. I'd fought my own logical mind on all of this for a year now. It had gotten harder and harder to deny her claims.

"Honestly, I don't know, but I guess I believe a little more with each clue I find and each case she helps us solve."

He laughed. "Well, maybe we should consider hiring her as a consultant. We could pitch it to the chief."

"Wow, that's... an idea... a bad idea, but an idea nonetheless."

"What did you tell Joanna about staying out here in Centerville for a few days?"

"Not much. Just we were working on a case that required us to partner with them. She's smart; I'm sure she would figure it out. Plus, all she cares about is that I'm back for that charity thing."

"If all goes right, you should make it back in time to change."

"True. What did you tell Whitney?"

"The same, but see with Whit, it's not withholding information. She doesn't know about the Senator, nor does she care. She only wants me safe and back home when I'm done."

"Good point. I've never lied to her or kept anything from her before. I have some guilt about it, but I had to."

"Why?"

"You know how she is. She'll do something stupid, like drive out here or get herself kidnapped."

"She does have a track record of that."

"My heart can't take that again."

We got to the CPD station and began the long process of going through every piece of evidence looking for clues. It was a lot of information and a lot of coffee, partnership, and cursing as we got dead end after dead end.

By the end of the week, we had more questions than answers, but I had to get back to Creekview for the charity event. So, I left the lead detective a list of things she should follow up on.

"I think this is a big one here and perhaps this one."

I didn't want to jinx myself, but we may have found two killers. If it was true, they were both a surprise and not who I thought it would be. I just needed Detective Vargas to help me finish connecting the dots and get the proof we needed to make it official.

For now, I had to focus on getting to this charity event and not letting anything slip about the investigation until I knew more. One wrong statement and Jo could be in danger, which was the last thing I wanted.

I also didn't want to tip off anyone that we knew. It could put the whole investigation in jeopardy. I had to get a win and I think if my hunch panned out, I would get the validation that I was good at my job after all.

Chapter Twenty-Nine

~ Joanna ~

It was finally the night of the fundraiser for Harper's Angels. The plan was for my parents to watch Oakley, Harris, and Dylan at my house, so all the couples were meeting here. We'd then take a limo to the event.

It had only been two weeks since Dad's accident, but the doctor had said he was healing well. However, he was still using crutches, so we all thought my house was easier for them because it was all one-story.

Though there aren't stairs, there are a few steps to the porch, which should be easy enough for Dad to handle. Then once in the front door, he can lay on the couch. He was mainly along just to keep Mom company anyway.

Plus, my house had all Oakley's things and was baby proof. Now with her just a few weeks from a year old, she was really moving around. Just this week, she'd learned to climb, which had been a challenge.

Unfortunately, my parent's house was not set up for a persistent toddler with no fear. Both their house and Audrey's were huge with stairs. Oakley would have a blast with those and with only Mom to chase them, it was just best at my house.

"Oh, Tessa, my hair looks fabulous." I looked at my reflection. "You outdid yourself this time!"

She had teased and poofed, sculpted, and twisted until my hair was in a perfect updo with delicate wisps of hair flowing and framing my face. She also did my makeup to highlight my high cheekbones and look almost natural.

Unfortunately, I couldn't return the favor, but her mother would do it for her. Ms. Ruby was even better at hair and makeup than her daughter.

"Alright, you're good. I'll be back later." Tessa said as she gave my hair a final spritz of hairspray.

"You never told me who your date is going to be."

"A new friend. His name is Mars." She said it so nonchalantly, as if it was no big deal.

She'd never mentioned him before, and in the years I'd known her, she'd never dated. I had no idea what to expect with Mars. I guess I'd soon find out.

"Mars. Okay. I can't wait to meet him."

After Tessa left, I got things ready for my parents. Given that all the care would be left to Mom, I wanted to ensure it was as easy for them to find things as possible. Audrey said she'd bring dinner for them so that Mom would just have to heat it up when they were ready.

Once that was done, I paced around as my nerves pulsed. Not much to do until it was time to slip on my dress. Oakley was asleep, and Chewy had already gotten a walk. He wouldn't get an evening one, but I had a nice-sized backyard, so it shouldn't be an issue.

"Do you want to go outside?"

Chewy barked and ran to the back door, so I grabbed a couple of his favorite balls and the baby monitor, and we went outside. It would wear him out and be a good excuse for me to pass the time.

While we were playing, Clint messaged that he was back in Creekview and couldn't wait to see me later.

Finally, Oakley woke up, so I had something to do. We played ball with Chewy. It was their favorite game and one neither of them tired of playing.

Once it was time to get dressed, I took her to my room and pulled out the mermaid-style floor-length gown. The plum-colored crystals around the neck of the gown cast a shiny sparkle around my room.

"Peetea!" Oakley squealed, reaching her chubby hands up to try to catch the dancing sparkles.

I stepped into the chiffon pile and then smoothed it over my curves. Then, turning to look in my full-length mirror, it fit perfectly. Not a wrinkle, roll, or line. Next, I slid into my silver strappy heels and grabbed my matching handbag.

I picked up my cell phone to snap a few pictures of myself, then scooped up Oakley to take a few with her. She was giggling while we took a few silly ones.

"Cheese!" I said.

"Eeeessseee." She copied.

There was a knock on the door that interrupted our moment.

"Let's go see who that is."

"Da?" She asked.

"Maybe."

I opened the door to see an incredibly sexy and handsome man in a tuxedo. His hair was styled slightly differently from his usual rolled out of bed look, clean-shaven with a giant smile.

"There are my girls." Clint said. "Whoa, Joanna, that dress... wow."

"And look at you, Mr. Sexy Detective."

He came in, kissing my cheek and Oakley's head. She launched herself at him.

"Da! Da!"

"Hey, baby girl."

As I prepared to shut the door, I saw Audrey, Stan, and their boys arriving, with Micah and Josh pulling up right behind them and my parents right behind them. No Tessa and Mars yet, but soon I would get to meet this mystery date. I couldn't wait.

I helped Audrey with getting the dinner settled in the kitchen. Stan and Clint helped Dad get comfortable on the couch. Everyone mingled and visited while we waited for the limo to arrive and the final couple.

"Have you met this guy that Tessa is bringing?" I asked Micah.

"Not yet. Until recently, I didn't even know about a guy, and she isn't giving up much information about him."

"Hm, I hope he is good enough for our Tessa." I joked.

"Well, I think she is a harsher critic of guys than we are." He laughed.

"Any wedding planning progress?"

"Don't ask me, ask Josh. He is now in charge of all of it."

"Sorry, sore subject?"

"With me? Not anymore." He frowned. "Did you know I'm a control freak?"

"That doesn't sound like my Micah."

He laughed. "Yeah, well, I just gave up all the control to my partner. I will just show up whenever and wherever he tells me."

"Well, okay, I'll talk to Josh about wedding stuff from now on."

Finally, there was a knock on the door, and the last couple arrived.

"Jo, Micah, this is my date. Mars." Tessa said as they stepped inside.

Gone was her usual goth girl look, and replaced was this elegant woman with long, silky straight black hair. Her makeup was simple and natural, much like how she had done mine, but just a slightly different hue to match her dark, almond shaped eyes. She was in a tea-length plum gown with black lace overlay with matching-colored strappy heels.

"Wow, Tessa, this dress is perfect for you." I said. "And, it's nice to meet you, Mars."

I finally took him in. He was a little taller than her by a few inches. He looked like a guy from one of those popular Korean boy bands. Handsome, clean-cut with a perfectly tailored suit that was the same color as her dress and a crisp white dress shirt under his jacket.

They were a stunning couple together and looked as if they had stepped right out of a fashion magazine.

"Nice to meet you as well. Hi, everyone." He addressed the room.

Behind them, I saw the limo pull up.

"Oh, limo is here," I said. "Mom, Dad, are y'all good?"

"We will be fine. Have fun, everyone." Mom called out.

We all headed outside, a parade of gorgeous men and beautiful women on our way to celebrate and enjoy an evening out. In the limo, we took selfies, laughed, and sipped champagne.

As we got close to the hotel that was hosting, we saw a long line of other limousines and town cars waiting to drop off patrons. I could just make out people disembarking from their cars, and they all looked glamorous and ready to partake in the night's festivities.

This would be my first time at this event, and they asked me to share my story at some point in the evening. Because of my speech, I had bought the table for our group to share in this special occasion. Plus, I wanted to make a nice donation to the charity.

"This is so exciting." Josh giggled.

"I feel like a celebrity." Micah said. "And it's not even about me."

"No, we're just lucky to be in the presence of a celebrity."
Clint said with a wink.

I blushed. I hated being the center of attention.

Finally, our limo reached the front of the line. Our door lined
up perfectly with the red carpet. Clint got out first and held his hand
for me. I took a deep breath before stepping out.

There was a photographer that snapped several pictures as
we got out and others as we made our way to the door.

"Wow, I feel like we're at some Hollywood party or premiere,"
Audrey said behind me.

"I know. This is crazy." I whispered back to her.

Inside, people mingled and greeted each other. There were
more photographers and dozens of hotel staff ready to direct people.
We simply followed the signs to the conference room.

"Name?" The doorman asked.

"Joanna Webber and party," I said.

"Webber... Webber... Ah, here you are. Table 20." He counted
each of us as we passed. "Enjoy." He smiled.

"Thank you." I nearly squealed as we made our way inside.

The room had been transformed from a plain conference
room to a luscious ballroom. The tables were draped with deep
crimson tablecloths then perfectly set with cream and gold place
settings. There were three glass vases on each table with twisty
branches suspended in the water and a silvery floating candle in
them.

"I see the table numbers are etched onto each vase." Audrey
pointed out.

"That's cute."

"An idea for our wedding, perhaps," Josh said to Micah. Micah
simply nodded.

"Did you pick a date yet?" I asked.

"September third." He gushed.

"Oh, wow! That's only a few months away."

"I know. We have so much to do, but I'll tell you everything
later." Josh said.

We arrived at our table, and once seated, waiters
immediately poured us drinks and handed us the menu for the
evening. We got a choice of one of three entrées: a filet mignon,

chicken breast, or an all-veggie option. All the meals were served with a salad first, then the steak and chicken could have a side of either a potato or steamed vegetables. Rolls with butter were brought to the table.

"Oh, there's Laney," I said as I waved to her. She waved then made her way to me.

"Hey, Jo. Everyone." She nodded around the table. I stood to give her a hug.

"You look stunning." She was wearing a navy-blue silky dress that hugged her slim figure. There was no bling or lace on her dress, but the sheen made it elegant and sexy.

"Thanks. So do you." She looked around the room. "This is quite the turnout, huh?"

"Yes, I am so glad I came."

"Me too."

"Who's your date?" I asked.

"Oh, just a guy... I'll fill you in later." She winked, then looked over her shoulder to him.

"I can't wait. We need to get together soon to plan the girls' birthday." I said.

"Yes, we do. I'll call you soon."

She hugged me once more and waved goodbye, returning to her hunky date. I watched her for a moment before returning to my seat and my own hot date.

After our dinners were served and eaten, various desserts were brought out on carts. We each selected something and got coffee. I selected a decadent chocolate cake with a few dark cherries topping it.

"Everything has been so delicious," I said to Clint as I pushed my dessert plate back. I'd nearly licked the plate clean. "That was the best chocolate cake I've ever eaten."

"The cheesecake was pretty good too." He said with a smile.

"Hello, everyone, and welcome." The MC greeted the crowd now that everyone had finished eating. "How about that wonderful meal?"

The crowd clapped.

"And can we get a round of applause for our gracious hosts and waitstaff?"

The crowd cheered and clapped again.

"I want to thank all our donors, both big and small; it all helps us continue our mission of placing families together. With your help, we have doubled our goal and reached a half-a-million dollars! So, give yourselves a round of applause."

Once again, the audience clapped.

The speech continued, and then she passed it over to the keynote, a child psychologist. She spoke, and then they played a slide show of families they'd helped. Among them was Oakley and I smiling in a picture taken at the park. Our social worker had taken it a couple of weeks ago at a visit.

"It's Oakley." Our table said in almost unison.

A few heads turned to smile at me, and I saw Laney turn towards me with a smile. I sure loved that little girl.

When the slide show concluded, they had another speaker. So, I took this opportunity to excuse myself to the ladies' room. I checked with the other ladies at the table, but nobody wanted to join me.

"I'll be right back." I smiled, kissing Clint before standing up.

I made my way through the room and out to the hallway. At first glance, I didn't see a sign for the ladies' room, so I wandered around. Finally, I found some tucked away in a quiet part of the hotel, so perhaps some were closer to the room. Oh well, I was here now.

Once I had used the facilities, I checked my reflection. I still looked pretty good. Of course, by now, my hair would start to go limp, and my makeup would start to run, but Tessa was really good at it, and for now, I was still put together.

"Well, well, who do we have here?" It was Vera.

"Hello, Vera. Your dress is stunning."

"Of course, it is." She snapped. "I have to look good for my fans."

At that moment, two large men came in behind her. A cold chill ran through me as I realized what was about to happen. I backed up a few steps, not sure where I would go. They grabbed me, and Vera stepped forward with a syringe.

"Enjoy your nap, Medium." She snickered as she jabbed the needle into my arm.

The room spun, and then everything went dark. My last thought was how hard I'd tried to stay out of danger this time. So much for that.

Chapter Thirty

~ Joanna ~

The next thing I knew, I was tied to a chair with large spotlights shining on me. My head was pounding, and the lights did not help. I squinted to try seeing around me better, but in addition to the pounding head, my vision was a bit blurry. I could only tell that we were in a large space, and behind the spotlights was darker as if the lights were only on us.

I wasn't sure how much time had elapsed between them taking me and me waking up here. It could have been minutes or days; I'd have no way to tell in this place.

I also quickly realized I was not alone here. Hank was next to me. So, when and where had they grabbed him, and how did they get him alone without Al?

He let out a painful moan.

"Hank... Hank... Are you okay?" I whispered.

"Joanna?" His voice was barely audible.

"Yes, I'm here."

I tried to determine where here was when I heard a voice from behind us. Vera. She'd changed from her evening gown into baggy sweatpants and a flowy crop top.

"Hey, my loyal followers, and welcome back to my live broadcast. As I said earlier, we were going to have two special guests today, and now that they are waking up from their nap, I want to introduce them. You probably don't know him, and honestly, I didn't know about him until a few days ago." She turned towards Hank.

"His father was my stepfather. When my stepfather died, he left all his money to him, Hank the Hammer. Money that should go to my mother, brother, and me, not someone who doesn't even need it. His name is Arnold Crawford, the second or how many around Creekview know him, Hank the Hammer Hammersley. For those outside of Creekview, he is the local mob boss, laundering money, shaking people down, and just being a royal pain." She looked over her shoulder and snarled at us.

She then looked back at the screen in front of her.

"Oh, hey, claire8181, yes, that's Joanna the Medium with a Heart right there. She's been helping Hank try to claim my inheritance. Can you believe it? He hasn't even been a part of this family, in like, ever, but I have been since I was 2 years old. That's right, MarcoNinja, 20 years and where was he? Not there. I had to put up with all the stupid family drama and commitments! The image of a Crawford. It's exhausting. I have to be on all the time, but I do love all you beautiful people." She blew kisses to the screen. "My point is, I earned that money."

She posed a few times, which seemed so random, but maybe it was to show off the handgun she was holding. I didn't know much about guns, but this one looked too heavy for her, and to top it off, she didn't look like she knew how to hold it safely.

"Um, Vera, what is going on here? What's your plan?" I asked.

"That's a good question." She glanced at her screen again. "One that a number of my followers are asking. Hey, chiapet1212, I see you, girl." She blew more kisses at the screen and then turned towards me with a menacing grin. "I plan to kill you both. Just like I did to his mother. After all, she killed his father... my stepfather. He was my hero, you know! At least until I found out the truth just days ago... he had a long-time affair with your mother, but she was never good enough to be with him as a wife. Not like my mother."

Hank growled next to me, but he still seemed pretty out of it. I guess they had given him more of the drug than they gave me, or perhaps they knocked him around a bit. I couldn't tell from this angle.

"I don't think you really want to do that, Vera," I said calmly. I had been held by people in the past, and I found that being calm was the key. "You're just upset."

"Hell, yeah, I'm upset. Upset that the two of you are trying to take what is mine and my mother's. She was married to that sloppy Senator for years and deserves to get millions. I loved him until I found out the truth about him. He was a disgusting excuse for a man in love with some old housekeeper." She cackled. "Just a mutt born to a housekeeper with no ties to anything."

Hank growled again and fought against his restraints. He tried to speak, but it mostly came out as slurred words.

"What was that, Hank the Hammer?" She manically laughed. "Oh, my dear followers, I love you and couldn't do this without you.

He's the reason why it was almost taken away. What would I do without your love?"

"It's not real love," I said.

"What did you say?" She advanced towards me, hitting me hard across the face with the gun. I yelped in pain. "They do love me. Many have said they would do anything for me, and I do mean anything."

She turned away and pointed behind the camera and lights to several shadowy figures I hadn't seen before. From their build and height, a few looked to be the ones that were with Vera in the restroom.

"These guys have been working with me for a while now. They love me and follow my every word. Whatever I ask, they do. They helped me kill Hank's housekeeper mother, and they killed the bodyguard when we picked this one up."

She pointed the gun at Hank.

"Al? Is Al dead?"

She laughed. "It looked that way, but I didn't stick around for his last breath. There sure was a lot of blood."

"You're an evil, horrible person. Why would anyone follow you?"

"Because I have money, and money is power." She snarled. "Plus, I'm pretty. I tell them what to buy, and they do it. Have you ever noticed when I use a product, it sells out? That lip gloss? They can't keep it in stock. Those pants, that hat, those shoes... They eat it up. Why? Because a beautiful girl with money said so."

"Why did you kill Hedy? What did she do to you?"

"I told you, she killed my stepfather!" She snapped. "If not for her, he would still be here today, and none of this would be in danger of being taken from me."

"Oh, Vera, that's crazy. Why would Hedy kill him? She loved him."

"I saw it! She was at the house that day. They had had lunch together, and she put something in his drink, I think. He suddenly swayed, and she had him lay down. Then she stood over him, claiming that he had led her on for years, denied her son, and she was here to get what was his. Next thing, she jabbed something into his neck. Then left."

Hank mumbled something next to me, but it was so slurred I couldn't make it out.

"Oh, Vera, that story... It's just your imagination."

"It's true. I saw it with my own eyes."

"Then why did you come to me and pretend you didn't know what happened that day?"

"Because I needed information and I thought if I could get his name, I'd never have to admit what I had done."

"No, it can't be true. I've spoken to her. She and Arnie are the ones that came to me in the first place. Together."

"No, it's not true... it's not." She stomped her foot, then looked at her screen and frowned. "Why are you all turning on me? She is the one and him. No, you're the idiot, not me. Fine, call the police. They will never find me." She said, replying to comments on her live stream.

"Yes, they may not be able to find you, but I knew right where to go." The voice of Irene Crawford came from the shadows.

"Mother? What are you doing here?"

"We were at the charity event, and they called Joanna to the stage, but she was missing." She turned towards me. "Then one of Hank's guys, I think he said his name was Eddie, found Al on the floor. He'll be okay. Just a bump on his head. He was taken to the hospital, just to be sure."

She came towards us, but Vera stepped in between, stopping Irene from getting close.

"Why are you messing this up, Mother? You always do this. You weren't a good enough wife, so Arnie didn't leave you his money, and now you are going to help them." Vera stomped her foot. "What about me? What about that money? I should be getting some of it."

"I am so sorry, Vera. I have not set the best example for you. I know that this social media thing has you so addicted to the likes and the compliments. All those people, they don't know you." At her mother's words, Vera gasped as if she'd been slapped.

Irene continued. "They only know this online version of you. But do they know the Vera that I know? The one that used to be so kindhearted, always thinking of others first. But it all changed when I bought you that first cell phone, and you started doing videos, then became so obsessed."

"I was just a little girl then, but I grew up. These people do love me. Look at these men back here... wait? Where did they go? How? Who?" She pointed the gun randomly, but as her hands started shaking, the gun suddenly appeared too heavy for her.

The men were gone and in their place was nearly the entire Creekview Police Department. They even had the canine units here.

"Vera, honey, please give me the gun. You don't want to hurt anyone, right?" Irene said softly. "I love you, baby. Please give me the gun."

"No, no! This can't... please, I need this." She glanced down at the screen and gasped, then screamed. "They are all gone. Everyone is gone."

She collapsed to the floor. As the gun slid out of her hand, I cringed, thinking it would go off. However, it slid harmlessly out of her hand.

She began sobbing loudly. The police rushed in, handcuffed her, and then took her out. While that happened, Clint, still dressed in his tux, stepped forward to help me out of my restraints, and Irene helped Hank.

"Jo, I was so scared when you didn't come back to the table, especially when they called your name as the next speaker. Then Eddie called about Al, and we started getting calls about Vera's live on all social media platforms." He pulled me to him and hugged me tightly.

"I'm so sorry. I was really careful this time." I said through my own sobs.

"You did. Well, you tried. I know." He kissed all over my face before reaching my lips.

After our quick kiss, I turned to see Hank being helped onto a stretcher and being attended to by EMTs. I tried to go to him, but my legs were weak.

"Is he okay?" I asked.

"He should be fine. He has a nice bump on his head, and we found the syringe they used to inject you both with. Seems to be lorazepam. It was just enough to knock you out, but he still feels it." One of the EMTs said.

"Oh, no, will we be okay?"

"Yes, but we will want to take you to the hospital as well. Just to check you out."

"What about everyone else? Where are they?" I asked in a panic.

"Audrey and Stan went home to relieve your parents. I sent everyone else home with a promise to give them an update once we had you safe."

They loaded me into the other ambulance, and Clint said he would meet me there. This nightmare was over, and thanks to the broadcast, they had Vera's full confession, including that she had killed Hedy.

But it still didn't answer the number one question: could Hedy really have killed Arnie like Vera said?

The question would have to be answered later because, for now, the focus was on ensuring Hank and I were okay.

Chapter Thirty-One

~ Joanna ~

It had been a few days since the kidnapping at the hands of Vera. The hospital checked me over, and I was fine. They kept me until morning to be safe. Hank had a bump to his head and had been given a slightly higher dose of the drugs than I was, so he spent an extra night in the hospital. Al received a few stitches and was released with antibiotics and a pain reliever.

Overall, we got off with a lot less serious injuries than in the past. I was so happy that I was simply able to walk out of the hospital.

We had the killer for Hedy, not for Arnie. Vera had said it was Hedy, but how could we confirm that? Clint said he had a few loose ends in Centerville and would be back today with what he hoped would be that answer.

He was being tight-lipped about what he was investigating and what he'd found so far. I'm not sure why, because even if it was Hedy, it wasn't like she could hurt me now. We were at the point for answers and closure, not to catch a killer.

I hadn't spoken to either Arnie or Hedy in a while. Arnie had been to see me just before the charity event, but Hedy hadn't been around in a few weeks. Did that mean she was guilty?

There was a knock at my door. I wasn't expecting company, but I went to peek. It was Hank.

"Hi, Hank, I wasn't expecting you."

"Hi, yes, I wanted to talk to you. You're the only one I know that will be honest with me."

"I will do my best." I stepped back and gestured. "Please come in. Something to drink?"

"Um, yes, just water, if it's not too much trouble." He sat in my living room, and Chewy plopped down at his feet. "Where is your beautiful daughter?"

"Oh, she's napping right now. Should be awake soon." I went into the kitchen and returned with a glass of ice water. "Here you are."

"Thank you." He sipped it. "Mm. I wanted to ask you... about that night with Vera. I was pretty out of it, and since the live stream was removed from the internet, I can't watch it. Not that I want to, after living through it, but did she really say she killed my mother?"

"That's what she said."

"Wow." He sat back. "I knew there was something not right about her death, but I could never prove it."

"Did you hear the part about why Vera said she did it?"

"No, if I did, I can't remember. Why?"

"She claims that Hedy killed Arnie."

"That can't be right." He sat forward and shook his head. "It's not possible."

"I know. I don't believe it either. She seems so sweet."

He stood, disturbing Chewy in the process, then began mumbling and pacing around my room. I wasn't sure if I should say anything, so I didn't. Instead, I waited patiently.

"My mother was a nice older lady. She attended book club, played bridge, ran 5Ks, and went to church. She wouldn't have killed someone. Could she?"

"I honestly don't know. You knew her better."

He bowed his head. "But even if she did, it isn't like... it isn't like they could charge her with anything. She's dead."

"Right, so you shouldn't let it change your opinion of her. She was your loving mother. That's all you need to remember."

He nodded and sat back down, staring straight ahead. I had a feeling this really did change a lot for him, though. I couldn't imagine how I would feel. It would be a mix of emotions, I'm sure. I could almost see them play across his face.

"But if this man was my father, she kept that from me. Not giving me a chance to know him, to meet him. She hid his identity from me and then killed him." His nostrils flared. "How could she do that?"

"I don't know. It's not fair to you or to him." Hank looked at me as a tear slid down his face. I took his hand. "I'm so very sorry, Hank."

He squeezed my hand. "Thank you for always being honest with me and trying to help. I know I wasn't always nice to you in the beginning of all this, but I think of you as family now."

"I feel the same."

As if on cue, in came Hedy right through my living room wall.

"Oh, Hedy, you're here."

Hank jumped. "Mother?"

"I'm here, son." As I spoke for her, she moved to his side. "I heard what Vera did to you. Are you okay?"

"I'm fine. Fine. She told me how you killed my father." It was the first time I had heard him call Arnold Crawford that.

"Oh, Hank, do you believe he is your father now? That's wonderful. You can go claim the money."

"The money? I don't want the money. But, heck, if I do decide to claim it, I'll just turn it over to the Crawfords. But I will never change my name. I've been Hank longer than I was Arnie the second."

"I did all this so you could have what's yours. The name and the money. You deserve both for what he did to us." I tried to add the fire in her tone, but I'm sure I fell short.

"So, you aren't denying you killed him?"

"No, why would I? I'm dead too. They can't do anything to me." She laughed, which I didn't translate. I just spoke the words and left it at that.

"How could you? Why would you do that?"

"Why are you so mad? Don't you order people to do the same thing? And isn't that how you started out?"

I can't say I was shocked. I sort of knew he did that, but to hear it said in words had me giving Hank a bit of side-eye. He could have had me killed when I stepped out of line and didn't follow his orders, but he didn't. He gave me a second and third chance, even coming to my rescue. It had me wondering about those he did kill or had killed, or if he really even did those things.

"He was my father, and you kept him from me, never told me, and then killed him before I ever had a chance to know him."

"He doesn't deserve your pity. He had many chances to step forward and be your father. He never took them, so when he told me about his will, I knew it was time to take action. So, I did what I had to do for you. I did it all for you."

"I can't believe you. This doesn't sound like you at all."

"There is so much you don't know about my life."

"Is there more?"

"Well, no, but I had friends and a life outside of you. I hated Arnie for what he did to us, so I took matters into my own hands. That is all."

"I can't. I just can't hear this anymore. We could go round and round, but I will never understand the why. I don't need money, so don't say it had anything to do with money. I make enough on my own."

"And how do you think that first bit of money came about? I gave you Crawford money to get started."

"Okay... well, but from there, I did it on my own. Yes, ten thousand dollars of seed money was great, but I have made millions since. And just to prove it, when I do claim the money, I will add back in twenty thousand of mine. Then hand it all over to Irene, Faye, Oren, and Viola. They all need it more than I do. Clearly, Irene will need it for legal fees."

"Hank, can you understand why I did it, at least?"

"No, honestly, I can't, and I don't want to hear any more about it. Sorry, Ms. Joanna, thank you for your time, but I'm leaving." He stood and walked straight out the door.

I stared at the closed door for a few moments after he had walked out, thankful that his slamming it hadn't woken Oakley. I turned to see Hedy. She was also staring at the closed door.

"Hedy, I think you should go now. With Hank knowing, our business is done." I said, tight-lipped.

"Yes, well, while that was a rude farewell, I still appreciate you passing on my messages all these weeks. We all have closure on this ugly chapter. Good day."

That was it. Hank had gotten to speak to his mother again and learned the truth about her death and her past. He met his father, sort of, and learned who he really was. But, I hoped, in some ways, it gave him peace.

I stood and carried Hank's glass into the kitchen. Rinsing it and then adding it to my dishwasher. I looked around. Nothing seemed important after that reading.

This case, more than any of the others, I had let myself get emotionally invested in the outcome. Probably because it was Hank. I really meant it when I told him I had started to think of him more as family. I truly cherished him and his men so much.

As I stood there, staring into space, a knock on the door pulled me from my thoughts. Chewy ran barking and spinning.

Peeking out, I saw it was Clint.

I flung the door open. "It was Hedy!" We said in unison.

"Wait, you know?" We again said together, causing us to laugh.

"You first," I said, pointing to him.

"Those clues I was chasing, I found out Hedy had bought the drugs, and we found the 'lost' security footage from Senator Crawford's house. It was Hedy."

"I just had her and Hank here. She confessed it all to him. She said she did it so he could claim his name and inheritance."

"Well, then our work here is done. I have the proof that we need legally, and you have the confession."

"We make a great team."

"We definitely do." He pulled me to him. "Should we get married?"

Before you go: If you loved Inherited Murder and haven't already received a copy of Unsolved Murder, the prequel to this series check out my website for the offer for your free novella.

www.ejwheltonwrites.com

Note by the Author:

Thank you for reading Inherited Murder. I hope you love Joanna, Clint, Hank, and the rest of the Creekview residents as much as I do. There are more stories coming from your favorite Medium.

Up next, we will visit Birdsong Senior Living Community where crafts and murder are among the amenities in Crafted Murder.

Then, we'll have Micah and Josh's destination wedding where love seems to be under attack when mysterious illnesses are making guests sick, and some never recover. That will be Destined Murder which may be the last book in the series. We shall see what the future of this series is.

I have other projects that I'm excited about them. More information will be available via my FaceBook, website, and through my newsletter.

To learn more visit: https://ejwheltonwrites.com/